THE WEREWOLF

LYCANTHROPY

By

MONTAGUE SUMMERS

This edition published by Read Books Ltd.
Copyright © 2019 Read Books Ltd.
This book is copyright and may not be
reproduced or copied in any way without
the express permission of the publisher in writing

British Library Cataloguing-in-Publication Data
A catalogue record for this book is available
from the British Library

CONTENTS

MONTAGUE SUMMERS

Augustus Montague Summers was born in Bristol, England in 1880. He was raised as an evangelical Anglican in a wealthy family, and studied at Clifton College before reading theology at Trinity College, Oxford with the intention of becoming a Church of England priest. In 1905, he graduated with fourth-class honours, and went on to continue his religious training at the Lichfield Theological College. Summers entered his apprenticeship as a curate in the diocese of Bitton near Bristol, but rumours of an interest in Satanism and accusations of sexual misconduct with young boys led to him being cut off; a scandal which dogged him his whole life. Summers joined the growing ranks of English men of letters interested in medievalism and the occult. In 1909, he converted to Catholicism and shortly thereafter he began passing himself off as a Catholic priest, the legitimacy of which was disputed. Around this time, Summers adopted a curious attire which included a sweeping black cape and a silver-topped cane.

Summers eventually managed to make a living as a full-time writer. He was interested in the theatre of the seventeenth century, particularly that of the English Restoration, and was one of the founder members of The Phoenix, a society that performed neglected works of that era. In 1916, he was elected a fellow of the Royal Society of Literature. Summers also produced some important studies of Gothic fiction. However, his interest in the occult never waned, and in 1928, around the time he was acquainted with Aleister Crowley, he published the first English translation of Heinrich Kramer and James Sprenger's *Malleus Maleficarum* ('*The Hammer of Witches*'), a 15th century Latin text on the hunting of witches. Summers then turned to vampires, producing *The Vampire: His Kith and Kin* (1928) and

The Vampire in Europe (1929), and then to werewolves with *The Werewolf* (1933). Summers' work on the occult is known for his unusual, archaic writing style, his intimate style of narration, and his purported belief in the reality of the subjects he treats.

In his day, Summers was a renowned eccentric; *The Times* called him *"in every way a 'character'"* and *"a throwback to the Middle Ages."* He died at his home in Richmond, Surrey.

THE WEREWOLF

LYCANTHROPY

AS old as time and as wide as the world, the belief in the werewolf by its very antiquity and its universality affords accumulated evidence that there is at least some extremely significant and vital element of truth in this dateless tradition, however disguised and distorted it may have become in later days by the fantasies and poetry of epic sagas, roundel, and romance. The ultimate origins of the werewolf are indeed obscure and lost in the mists of primeval mythology, and when we endeavour to track the slot too far we presently find ourselves mused and amazed, driven to hazard and profitless conjecture, unless we are sensible enough to recognize and candid enough to acknowledge the dark and terrible mysteries, both psychic and physical, which are implicated in and essentially permeate a catena of evidence past dispute, and which alone can adequately explain or account for the prominence and the survival of those cruel narratives which have come down to us throughout the centuries, and the facts of which are being repeated to-day in the evil-haunted depths of African jungles, and even in remoter hamlets of Europe, farmy woods and mountain vales, almost divorced from the ken of man and wellnigh unvisited by civilization.

The mere somatist; the rationalist, often masquerading nowadays under Christian credentials; the rationalizing anthropologist; the totemist; the erratic solarist; "prompt to impose and fond to dogmatize," each and every, in his hot-paced eagerness to expiscate and explain the manner of all mysteries in earth and heaven, will not be slow to broach and argue his newest superstitions, the fruit of trivially profound research, vagaries which can neither interest, instruct, nor yet entertain the true scholar of simpler vision and clearer thought, since in the end these veaking inquirers commonly arrive at nothing, and like the earth-born sons of Cadmean tilth it has proved in the past that again and again do they painfully destroy themselves by internecine war.

Yet there may be found some in whom the missionary spirit of error is so pertinacious that they will refurbish and seemingly with intenser conviction reiterate sham theories a thousand times discredited and disproved. Thus, with regard to the very subject of the werewolf, which he only touches quite cursorily as he passes by, Sir William Ridgeway in his *Early Age of Greece* was constrained to warn the student that he "must be careful lest whilst he is avoiding the Scylla of solar mythology, he may be swallowed up in the Charybdis of totemism",[1]

Precisely to define the werewolf is perhaps not altogether easy. We may, however, say that a werewolf is a human being, man, woman or child (more often the first), who either voluntarily or involuntarily changes or is metamorphosed into the apparent shape of a wolf, and who is then possessed of all the characteristics, the foul appetites, ferocity, cunning, the brute strength, and swiftness of that animal. In by far the greater majority of instances the werewolf to himself as well as to those who behold him seems completely to have assumed the furry lupine form. This shape-shifting is for the most part temporary, of longer or shorter duration, but it is sometimes supposed to be permanent. The transformation, again, such as it is, if desired, can be effected by certain rites and ceremonies, which in the case of a constitutional werewolf are often of the black goetic kind. The resumption of the original form may also then be wrought at will. Werewolfery is hereditary or acquired; a horrible pleasure born of the thirst to quaff warm human blood, or an ensorcelling punishment and revenge of the dark Ephesian art.

It should be remarked that in a secondary or derivative sense the word werewolf has been erroneously employed to denote a person suffering from lycanthropy, that mania or disease when the patient imagines himself to be a wolf, and under that savage delusion betrays all the bestial propensities of the wolf, howling in a horrid long-drawn note. This madness will hardly at all concern us here. Werewolf is also in one place[2] found to specify an exceptionally large and ferocious wolf, and according to Dr. John Jamieson, in the county of Angus, Warwolf, pronounced *warwoof*, was anciently used to designate a puny child, or an ill-grown person of whatever age.[3]

Verstegan, that is to say, Richard Rowlands,[4] in his *A Restitution of Decayed Intelligence*, 4to, 1605, has: "Were our ancestors vsed somtyme in steed of *Man* yet should it seeme that *were* was moste commonly taken for a maried man. But the name of *man* is now more knoun and more generally vsed in the whole Teutonic toung then the name of *Were*.

"*Were-wulf*. This name remaineth stil knoun in the Teutonic, & is as much to say as *man-wolf*, the greeks expressing the very lyke, in *Lycanthropos*.

"*Ortelius*[5] not knowing what *were* signified, because in the *Netherlandes* it is now clean out of vse, except thus composed with *wolf*, doth mis-interpret it according to his fancie.

"The *were-wolves* are certaine sorcerers, who hauing annoynted their bodyes, with an oyntment which they make by the instinct of the deuil; and putting on a certaine inchanted girdel, do not only vnto the view of others seeme as wolues, but to their oun thinking haue both the shape and nature of wolues, so long as they weare the said girdel. And they do dispose thēselues as very wolues, in wurrying and killing, and moste of humaine creatures.

"Of such sundry haue bin taken and executed in sundry partes of *Germanie*, and the *Netherlands*. One *Peeter Stump*[6] for beeing a *were-wolf*, and hauing killed thirteen children, two women, and one man; was at *Bedbur*[7] not far from *Cullen* in the year 1589 put vnto a very terrible death. The flesh of diuers partes of his body was pulled out with hot iron tongs, his armes thighes & legges broke on a wheel, & his body lastly burnt. He dyed with very great remorce, desyring that his body might not be spared from any torment, so his soule might be saued. The *were-wolf* (so called in *Germanie*) is in *France*, called Loupgarov."

This "etymological explanation", says Professor Ernest Weekley in his *More Words Ancient and Modern*,[8] "is substantially correct." This authority remarks that strictly *were* "should be *wer*, a word of wider diffusion in the Aryan languages than *man* or *gome*. It is found in all the Teutonic languages and is cognate with Lat. *vir*, Gaelic *fear*, Welsh *gŵr*, Sanskrit *vīra*. *Were* died out in early Mid. English, but survives historically in *wergild*".[9] He also adds: "The disappearance of the simple *were* led Mid. English writers to explain the first syllable as *ware*, and, as late as 1576, Turberville tells us, 'Such wolves are called "warwolves", bicause a man had neede to be ware of them.'[10] A similar idea seems to account for archaic Ger. *wehrwolf*, associated with the cognate *wehren*, to protect, take heed."

As Verstegan notes, the Greek λυκάνθρωπος is a word-formation exactly corresponding to the Anglo-Saxon *were-wulf*, which occurs as a synonym for the devil in the laws of King Cnut, Ecclesiastical Ordinances, xxvi. "Thonne moton tha hyrdas beon swydhe wacore and geornlice clypigende, the widh thonne theodsceadhan folce sceolan scyldan, thaet syndon biscopas and maessepreostas, the godcunde heorda bewarian and bewarian sceolan, mid wislican laran, thaet se wodfreca werewulf to swidhe ne slyte ne to fela ne abite of godcundse heorde." "Therefore must be the shepherds be very watchful and diligently crying out, who have to shield the people against the spoiler; such are bishops and mass-priests, who are to preserve and defend their spiritual flocks with wise instructions, that the madly audacious were-wolf do not too widely devastate, nor bite too many of the spiritual flock."[11]

It is interesting to remark that Werwulf actually occurs as a proper name, since Asser in his *De Rebus Gestis Ælfredi* mentions "Æthelstan quoque et Werwulfum, sacerdotes *et capellanos*, Mercios genere, eruditos, "who helped that monarch in his studies, and were duly rewarded by him."[12]Werwulf, the Mercian priest, was a friend of Bishop Werfrith of Worcester, and the name is found in various charters, some of which, however, are by no means altogether above suspicion. One may compare such names as Ethelwulf, "the Noble Wolf"; Berthwulf, "the Illustrious Wolf"; Eadwulf, "the Prosperous Wolf"; Ealdwulf, "the Old Wolf," and many more.

Bishop Burchard of Worms, who died in August, 1025, in the nineteenth Book, *De Poenitentia*, of his *Decreta*—"Liber hic Corrector vocatur et Medicus"[13]—instructs the priest to ask a penitent the following: "Credidisti quod quidam credere soient, ut illae quae a vulgo parcae vocantur, ipsae, vel sint, vel possint hoc facere quod creduntur; id est, dum aliquis homo nascitur, et tunc valeant ilium designare ad hoc quod velint ut quandocunque ille homo voluerit, in lupum transformari possit, quod vulgaris stultitia weruvolff vocat, aut in aliam aliquam figuram? Si credidisti, quod unquam fieret aut esse possit, ut divina imago in aliam formam aut in speciem transmutari possit ab aliquo, nisi ab omnipotente Deo, decem dies in pane et aqua debes poenitere."[14]

It must be here carefully remarked that Burchard's question does not for a moment imply any doubt as to the reality of the demon werewolf. In a sense it cuts deeper than that. The essential point of the priest's query is whether the person seeking absolution has doubted the omnipotence of Almighty God, has sinfully allowed himself to wonder whether the powers of evil may not wellnigh match the powers of good, and thus be able to perform diabolic miracles and marvels in despite, as it were, of the Supreme Deity. This, of course, is the deadly error of the Manichees, the dualism of good and evil, a divided empire. During the twelfth century Western Europe, in particular Italy, France, and Germany, suffered from an extraordinary outburst of dualism, the adherents of which foul doctrines propagated their dark creed with tireless zeal until the country began to swarm with Catharists, Albigenses, Paterini, Publicani, Bulgari, Tisserands, Bougres, Paulicians, and a thousand other subversive sectaries.[15] The ultimate principle of these beliefs, differ as they might in detail, was Satanism. Raoul Glaber, a monk who died at Cluny about 1050, writing his contemporary *History*, speaks of their obstinate persistence in these abominations: "Hos nempe cunctos ita maculaverat haeretica pravitas, ut ante erat illis crudeli morte finiri, quam ab illa quoquomodo possent ad saluberrimam Christi Domini fidem revocari. Colebant enim idola more paganorum, ac cum Iudaeis inepta sacrificia litare nitabantur."[16]

Nearly three centuries earlier than Burchard, S. Boniface, the martyred Archbishop of Mayence, Apostle of Germany, in his sermon *De abrenuntiatione in baptismate*,[17] "concerning those things which a Christian renounceth at his Baptism," speaks of "veneficia, incantationes et sortilegos exquirere, strigas et fictos lupos credere, abortum facere", that is to say, "poisonings, magic spells and the curious seeking out of lots, trusting implicitly in witches and a superstitious fear of werewolves, the procuring of abortion, as among the 'mala opera diaboli', 'the abominable works of the devil.'" The Saint classes these sins with "superbia, idololatria, invidia, homicidium, detractio, . . . fornicatio, adulterium, omnis pollutio, furta, falsum testimonium, rapina, gula, ebrietas . . .", "pride, the worshipping of idols, envy, murder, malice, . . . fornication, adultery, all uncleanness, theft, false witness, despoiling by violence, gluttony, drunkenness, . . . ," and other evil deeds. The phrase "strigas et fictos lupos credere" does not mean merely "to believe that witches and werewolves exist", but "to put one's trust in the power of sorcerers and to believe that the devil is able of his own might to transform men into wolves", which is to say one gives the glory to Satan rather than to God, as in truth witches and warlocks use and are wont.

The word werewolf in its first and correcter signification is employed by Gervase of Tilbury, who in his *Otia Imperialia* thus explains the term: "Vidimus enim frequenter in Anglia per lunationes homines in lupos mutari, quod hominum genus *gerulfos* Galli nominant, Anglici vero *werewlf* dicunt: *were* enim Anglice *virum* sonat, *wlf* lupum."[18]

Gervase of Tilbury composed his *Otia* about 1212, and rather more than a century later in the English poem *William of Palerne*, otherwise known as the Romance of "William and the Werwolf", translated from the twelfth century *Roman de Guillaume de Palerne* at the command of Sir Humphrey de Bohun[19] about 1350, we have the word *werwolf*, as in 11. 79–80:—

> For i wol of þe werwolf a wile nov speke.
> Whanne þis werwolf was come to his wolnk denne . . .

and the word is not infrequently repeated throughout the poem.[20]

The following lines occur in *Pierce the Ploughmans Crede*[21](*c.* 1394):—

> In vestimentis ouium, but onlie wiþ-inne þei ben wilde wer-wolues þat wiln þe folk robben. þe fend founded hem first . . .

The Vulgate, secundum Matthæum, vii, 15, has: "Attendite a falsis prophetis, qui veniunt ad vos in vestimentis ovium, intrinsecus autem sunt lupi rapaces." The Douai translation runs: "Beware of false prophets, who come to you in the clothing of sheep, but inwardly they are ravening wolves." The Authorized Version is practically identical: "Beware of false prophets which come to you in sheep's clothing, but inwardly they are ravening wolves." The Revised is the same. The original Greek has λύκοι ἅρπαγες for the words translated "ravening wolves" or in *Pierce the Ploughmans Crede* "wer-woules". Here, too, they seem to be regarded as definitely inspired by the demon, although this detail perhaps should not be pressed.

In Sir Thomas Malory's *Le Morte Darthur*, which was completed about 1470, book xix, c. xi, mention is found of "Sir Marrok the good knyghte that was bitrayed with his wyf for she made hym seuen yere a werwolf".[22]

Among Scottish poets Robert Henryson, who was born about the beginning of the second quarter of the fifteenth century and who died certainly not later than 1508, in his *Morall Fabillis of Esope the Phrygian*, "Compylit in Eloquent, and Ornate Scottis Meter," in "The Trial of the Fox", writes:—

> The Minotaur, ane Monster meruelous,
> Bellerophont, that beist of Bastardrie,
> The Warwolf, and the Pegase perillous,
> Transformit be assent of sorcerie . . .[23]

In *The Flyting of Dunbar and Kennedie*,[24] the latter poet addresses his rival in the following terms:—

> Dathane deuillis sone, and dragon dispitous,
> Abironis birth, and bred with Beliall;
> Wod werwolf, worme, and scorpion vennemous,
> Lucifers laid, fowll feyindis face infernall;
> Sodomyt, syphareit fra sanctis celestiall, . . .[25]

Alexander Montgomerie in his *Flyting of Montgomerie and Polwart* (1582),[26] has:—

> Ane vairloche, ane woirwolf, ane wowbat of hair,
> Ane devill, and ane dragoun, ane doyed dromodarie, . . .[27]

A little earlier in the same poem he reviles his adversary:—

> With warwoolffs and wild cates thy weird be to wander;[28]

In the excellent old comedy *Philotus*[29] young Flavius thus

14

conjures and exorcises Emily:—

> Throw power I charge the of the Paip,
> Thow neyther girne, gowl, glowme, nor gaip,
> Lyke Anker saidell, like unsell Aip,
> Lyke Owle nor Alrische Elfe:
> Lyke fyrie Dragon full of feir,
> Lyke Warwolf, Lyon, Bull nor Beir,
> Bot pas thow hence as thow come heir,
> In lykenes of thy selfe.[30]

King James VI of Scotland in his *Dœmonologie*, 1597, iii, 1, has "war-woolfes" and "λυκανθρωποι which signifieth men-woolfes".

John Sibbald in the Glossary to his *Chronicle of Scottish Poetry* has: "Warwolf, according to an antient vulgar idea, *a person transformed to a wolf.* Teut. *weer wolf,* Swed. *warulf,* lycanthropus; hoc est, qui ex ridicula vulgi opinione in lupi forma noctu obambulat. Goth. *vair,* vir; & *ulf,* lupus. It is not unlikely that *Warlock* may be a corruption of this word."[31] This is, of course, a wholly impossible etymology since the first element in *Warlock* is the O.E. *wœr* "covenant"; and the second element is related to O.E. *leogan* "to lie or deny".[32] Thus the first meaning of *Warlock* is one who breaks a treaty, the violator of his oath, a man forsworn; hence in general a false and wicked person, and then a magician, a sorcerer.

In the famous "Discourse of Witchcraft as it was acted in the Family of Mr. Edward Fairfax", 1621, occurs another form of the word werewolf. "Above all [the transformation of] the Leucanthopoi is most miraculous . . . which Witches that people do call *weary wolves*."

The modern German is Werwolf, which has a less correct old form Währwolf. There are variants, and also corruptions such as bärwolf, which is given in Johann Georg Wachter's *Glossarium Germanicum*,[33] berwolff in Camerarius,[34] and berwulf.[35]

Werwolf, notes Wachter, "componitur a *wer* vir, & *wolf*

lupus. Et dicitur etiam *bær-wolf*, quia alia Dialectio *bar* est vir. Galli alio & meliori compositionis ordine vocant *loupgarou*. Nam proprie est homo in lupum mutatus, non lupus homini infestus. De Gallica voce mire nugantur eruditi. *Garou*virum denotare, iam supra demonstravi in *gur* vir. Cæterum homines in lupos transformari, vetustissima fama est . . . Patet . . . hanc transmutationem secundum antiquam credulitatem non fuisse morbum, sed rem liberam & voluntariam."[36]

Eugen Mogk in an article entitled *Der Werwolf*, which he contributed to Hermann Paul's *Grundriss der Germanischen Philologie*, writes: "Die Bedeutung des Wortes ist klar: *wer* = Mann, Werwolf also der Mann in Wolfsgestalt."[37]

Oskar Schrade in his *Altdeutsches Wörterbuch*[38] draws attention to *wërwolf* (*mittelhochdeutsch*) and *werawolf* (*althochdeutsch*). There is a West Frisian *waerûl* and *warûle*, as also a form *waerwulf*, which latter is derived from the Middle Dutch (and Modern) *weerwolf*. Franz Passow in his *Handwirterbuch der Griechischen Spreche*, Leipzig, 1852, under λυκάνθρωπος (ii, p. 89), notes the Dutch *ghierwolf*. The Gothic has *vairavulfs*. The Danish and Norwegian *varulv* and Swedish *varulf* are, it has been suggested, formed on a Romance or German model. *Varulf*, indeed, may be connected with an Old Norman *varulf*.

The Icelandic *vargr* denotes a wolf, and *vargúlfr*, literally a "worrying wolf", means a werewolf. Vigfusson quotes from Unger's edition of *Strengleikar* (*Lays of the Britons*),[39] "bisclaret í Bretzku máli en Norðmandingar kallaðu hann vargúlf," and "v. var eitt kvikindi meðan hann býr í vargsham," upon which he comments: "This word [*varg-úlfr*], which occurs nowhere but in the above passage, is perhaps only coined by the translator from the French *loup-garou* qs. *gar-ulf*; *ver-úlfr*[40] would have been the right word, but that word is unknown to the Icelandic or old Norse, the superstition being expressed by *eigi ein-hamr, ham-farir, hamast*, or the like."[41] *Ham-farir* signifies "the '*faring*' or *travelling* in the assumed shape of an animal, fowl or deer, fish or serpent, with magical speed over land and sea, the wizard's own body meantime lying lifeless and motionless".[42]

On the French word *loupgarou* Littré has the following etymological note: "Wallon, *leu-warou*, *léwarou*; Hainaut *léuwarou*; Berry *loup berou*, *loup brou*; picard, *leuwarou*; norm, *varou*, loup garou, *varouage*, course pendant la nuit (*garouage* se dit avec le même sens parmi les paysans des environs de Paris); bourguig. *leu-voirou*; bas-lat. *gerulphus*, loup-garou. Gerulphus a donné *garwall*, *garou*; c'est donc *gerulphus* qu'il faut étudier; il réprésente l'anglo-saxon *vere wolf*; danois *var-ulv*; suédois, *var-ulf*, qui étant composé de *ver*, *vair*, homme, et de *wolf*, *ulf*, loup, signifie *homme-loup*. La locution *loup-garou* est donc un pléonasme où *loup* se trouve deux fois, l'un sous la forme française, l'autre sous la forme germanique. *Verewolf* est, on le voit, un mot composé semblable à λυκάνθρωπος. Au germanique *ver*, comparez *vir*, ἥρως, en sanscrit *vīra*, homme fort, et en celtique *ver*, homme."[43]

Fréderic Godefroy, *Dictionnaire de l'Ancienne Langue Française*,[44] gives: "Garol, garwall, guaroul, wareul, varol, s.m. esprit malin que l'on supposait errer la nuit transformé en loup.

> Quant de lais faire m'entremet
> Ne voil ublier Bisclaveret;
> Bisclaveret ad nun en Bretan,
> *Garwall* l'apelent li Norman.
> (Marie, *Lai du Bisclaveret*, 1, Roq.)
> Et si a tant garous et leus.
> (G. de Coinci, *Mir.*, MS. Soiss., f° 24a.)[45]
> Que nous deffende, que nous gart
> De ces *guarous* et de ce leus.
> (Id. *ib.*, f° 24b.)
> Que n'est lions, *wareus* ne leus.
> (Id. *ib.*, f° 173n.)
> Lou *garol*.
> (Id. *ib.*, MS. Brüx., f° 23d.)

Et au *guaroul* qui les engine.
(G. de Palerme. Ars. 3319, f° 108 vo.)

Haut-Maine, *gairou*. Norm., Guernesey, *varou*."[46]
Godefroy's quotation from the *Lai du Bisclaveret* does not, however, supply the best text which is to be found in the British Museum MS., Harley 978,[47] and which begins as follows:—

Quant de lais faire mentremet
Ne uoil ublier bisclaueret
Bisclaueret ad nun en bretan
Garwaf lapelent li norman.

Garwaf is then the Norman equivalent of the Breton *bisclaveret*. In his *Dictionnaire François-Celtique ou François-Breton*, Rennes, 1732, the learned Capuchin Gregoire de Rostrenen has: "Loup-garou. Bleiz-garv. bleiz-garo. *p.* bleizy-garo (garo, *âpre, cruel.*) den-vleiz. *p.* tud-vleiz. gobylin. *p.* goblinad. (gobilin, *veut dire esprit folet nocturne.*) *Van.* bleidet, un deen bleydet. tud bleydet."[48] In Breton there also exists the term *den-bleiz; den* meaning a man, and *bleiz* signifying wolf.

Bodin in his *Demonomanie des Sorcius*, ii, 6, in his chapter on werewolves writes: "Les Alemans les appellent Vver Vvòlf, & les François loups garous; les Picards loups varous, comme qui diroit *lupos varios*, car les François mettent g. pour v. Les grecs les appelloyent Lycanthropes, & Mormolycies; Les Latins les appelloyent *vorios & versipelles*, comme Pline a noté parlant de ce changement de loups en hommes. François Phoebus Conte de Foix, en son luire de la Chasse, diet que ce mot Garoux, veut dire gardez vous, dequoy le President Fauchet m'a aduerty."[49]

Gaston III de Foix (Phébus) was born in 1331 and died 1391. *Le miroyr de Phebus des deduicts de la chasse aux Bestes sauluaiges Et des oyseaulx de proye* is one of the most famous medieval treatises of venery,[50] and the passage to which Bodin refers may be found in chapter x, "Cy devise du loup et de toute sa nature."

"Il y a aucuns qui manguēt des enfās et aucūesfois les hommes et ne māguent nulle autre chair depuis qu'ils sont encharnes aux hommes aincois se laissent mourir et ceux on appelle loups garous: car on fendoit garder."

The learned Capuchin Jacques d'Autun in his *L'Incredulité Sçavante et la Credulité Ignorante*, Lyon, 1678, Troisième Partie, Discours xxx (p. 904), writes: "On voit des Sorciers en forme de Loups se ietter sur les hommes, plustost que sur les bestes; c'est la raison, dit vn Comte de Foix, pourquoy on les appelle *Loups-garoux*, c'est à dire *gardez vous*: parce que leur rage les porte à esgorger & à courir s'ils peuuent sur les personnes qu'ils rencontrent, & s'ils sont repoussés, on les voit tourner leur furie sur les Troupeaux, où ils font d'estranges rauages."

This curious etymology passed into English, being seriously put forward (as already noted) by Turberville, who derived it from the English treatise *The Booke of huntynge* or *Master of game* (*c.* 1400), chapter vii, "Of ye Wolf and of his nature." The passage runs: "ther ben some that eten chyldren & men and eteth noon other flesh fro that tyme that thei be a charmed with mannys flesh, ffor rather thei wolde be deed. And thei be cleped Werewolfes for men shulde be war of hem."[51]

Frédéric Mistral, in his *Dictionnaire Provençal-Français*,[52] records many variants of the word *loup-garou* which appears in differing dialects as *loup-garoun, loup-carou, louparou, louppaumè, loup-berou, loubérou, leberou, garuló*. In Limousin are found *leberoun* and *leberou*. In Dauphiné a werewolf is *lamiaro*. The word *brouch* (sometimes *borouch*) also means a werewolf, although it is more generally employed to denote a wizard, a sorcerer. Cotgrave in his *Dictionarie of the French and English Tongues*, 1611, defines *loup-garou* as "*A mankind Wolfe; such a one as once being flesht on men, and children will rather starue then feed on any thing else; also, one that, possesed with an extreame, and strange melancholie, beleuues he is turned Wolfe, and as a Wolfe behaues himselfe*".

The Italian term for a werwolf is *lupo mannaro* or *mannaro*;

the Portuguese *lobis-homem* or *lycanthropo*.[53] In Spain the word is *lobombre*.[54]

In the Sicilian dialect there are many variants of *lupo mannaro*, among the more common being *lupunàru*, *lupunàriu*, *lupuminàru*, *lupuminariu* (Messina), *lupupunàru* (Franco-fonte), *lupupinàru* (Naso), *lupucumunàriu* (Piazza), *lupitiminàriu* (Nicosia), *daminàr* (San Fratello), and many more.

Although ancient Greek mythology affords innumerable stories of animal metamorphoses, amongst others it will be readily remembered that Homer describes the witch-queen Circe as surrounded by a strange pack of human animals—

Ἀμοὶ δε μιν λύκοι *σαν ὀρέστεροι ἠδὲ λέοντες,
Τοὺς αὐτὴ κατέθελξεν, ἐπεὶ κακὰ οάρμακ' ἔδωκεν,[55]

and the story of Lycaon is of dateless antiquity, yet the word λυκάνθρωπος is not of early occurrence, whilst the poem of Marcellus Sidetes, who lived in the reigns of Hadrian and Antoninus Pius, A.D. 117–161, Περὶ λυκανθρώπου,[56] deals with the disease lycanthropy. Paul Ægineta, whose extant work is conveniently known as *De Re Medica Libri Septem*,[57] probably flourished in the latter half of the seventh century. He employs the term λυκανθρωπία, the disease. Galen mentions the νόσος κυνάνθρωπος[58] (a cognate formation), in which malady the patient imagines himself to be a dog, and the grammarian Joannes Tzetzes in his *Chiliades* terms the Minotaur βοάνθρωπος.[59]

E. A. Sophocles in his *Greek Lexicon of the Roman and Byzantine Periods*, 146 B.C.–A.D. 1100 (Havard University Press, 1914), records λυκανθρωπία as "lycanthropy", and λυκάνθρωπος as one afflicted with lycanthropy. He does not appear to recognize the meaning werewolf.[60]

Reginald Scot in his notorious *Discouerie of witchcraft*, book v, expresses his agreement with "such physicians, as saie that *Lycanthropia* is a disease, and not a transformation".[61] He has in this passage merely transliterated the Greek. Nathan Bailey in his *Universal Etymological English Dictionary* (8vo, 1721) has: "Werewolf, [Werwolf or Werewolff, Teut. q.d. *A Man-Wolf,* or *Wolf-Man;* λυκάνθρωπος, Gr.] a Sorcerer, who by means of an inchanted Girdle, &c. takes upon hims the Shape and Name of a Wolf." He also notes: "Lycanthropy. [*Lycanthropie,* F. *lycanthropia.* L. of λυκανθρωπία, Gr.] a madness proceeding from the Bite of a Mad Wolf, wherein men imitate the Howling of Wolves." Dr. Johnson does not notice "Werewolf" but under Lycanthropy[62] he has: "[lycantropie, French; λύκαν and ἄνθρωπος.] A kind of madness, in which men have the qualities of wild beasts.

"He sees like a man in his sleep, and grows as much the wiser as a man that dreamt of a *lycanthropy,* and was for ever after wary not to come near a river.—*Taylor.*"

At some indeterminate period the word λυκάνθρωπος fell into disuse among the Greeks and its place was taken by λυκοκάντζαρος. It is quite possible, of course, that even to-day λυκάνθρωπος may be employed in some obscure and obsolescent dialect, but the only place where it seems to be definitely recorded of late is in a tale given by J. G. von Hahn in his collection *Griechische und albanesische Märchen,*[63] The variant of this particular story comes from Attica, and Hahn draws especial attention to λυκάνθρωπος, which in his German version he renders by the unusual "Der Wolfsmann".

In λυκοκάντζαρος the second element κάντζαρος is the modern form of κένταυρος, and is most commonly known from its combination καλλικάντζαροι.[64] Since the Callicantzari will be described and discussed in the chapter dealing with the werewolf in Greece, it is sufficient here to note that to-day in the few districts (chiefly Cynouria, Messenia, and Crete) where λυκοκάντζαρος is still to be heard, the meaning has changed, and so far from signifying a werewolf, a man transformed to a beast, it almost invariably denotes the καλλικάντζαρος himself, who is generically a grotesque and dangerous demon of no human origin, a bugaboo, sometimes appearing in man's shape and sometimes completely metamorphosed as a hideously fantastic and savage monster.

Antoine Th. Hépitès in his *Lexicon Hellenogallicon*,[65] Athens, 1909, has: "λυκανθρωπία . . . lycanthropie, n.f. μελαγχολικὴ ἀσθένια καθ᾽ ἥν ὁ ἀσθενὴς περιOέρεται τὴν νύκτα καὶ ὠρύεται ὡς λύκος." Apparently he only recognizes the word λυκανθρωπία as denoting the disease, and not equivalent to werewolfery. Under λυκάνθρωπος however, he notes: "lycanthrope. n.m. (κυρ. ὁ λαμβάνων τὸ σχῆμα καὶ τὴν Οωνήν τοῦ λύκου), ὁ πάσχων ἀπὸ λυκανθρωπίαν [συνεκδ.] ἀγριάνθρωπος, homme-sauvage, n.m. loup-garou, n.m." Ἀγριάνθρωπος, however, conveys little (if anything) more than the English wildman, and under this word Hépitès records[66]: "ὁ μὴ πεπολιτισμένος, homme sauvage; μισάνθρωπος, ἀκοινώνητος, loup-garou," whilst in the French-Greek section of his work he defines: "Loup-garou. ἐσ. ἀρσ. ΜτΟ. "Ανθρωπος περιπλανώμενος τὴν νυκτά ἐν μορΟῆ λύκου κατὰ τοὺς δεισιδαίμονας. λυκάνθρωπος, ὁ ἀγριάνθρωπος, καὶ ἐν γένει ὁ μισάνθρωπος[67] It is clear that the correct and original meaning werewolf is tending to become merely metaphorical and at last to signify nothing more than a misanthrope or a surly fellow.

The ordinary Greek word for a vampire is βρυκόλακας, *vrykólakas*, and this has a long and interesting history, being derived in the first place from a Slavonic word which in all Slavonic languages save one—the Serbian—is the exact equivalent of werewolf. Franz Miklosich has the following account in his *Etymologisches Wörterbuch der Slavischen Sprachen*[68]: "velkŭ, Old Slav., vlъkъ *wolf* . . . Old Slav., vlъkodlakъ *vulcolaca*: . . . Slovenian, volkdlak, vukodlak, vulkodlak; Bulgarian, vrъkolak; Kr., vukodlak; Serb., vukodlak; Cz., vlkodlak; Pol., wilkolak; Little Russian, volkolak, volkun; White Russian, volkolak; Russian, volkulaktъ; Roum., ve.lkolak, ve.rkolak; Alb., vurvolak; Modern Grk., βουλκόλακα, βρουκόλακας; Lith., vilkakis; Lett. vilkats. *Man beachte lit.* vilktrasa *werwolf. Der* vlъkodlakъ *ist der Werwolf der Deutschen, woraus mlat.* guerulfus, *mannwolf, der in wolfsgestalt gespenstich umgehende mann: vergl. Neuri in terra Tatarorum, qui mutari possunt in lupos."*

The second element in the word is perhaps to be identified with *dlaka*, meaning a "hair" (of an animal, generally a cow or horse), a word found in Old Slav., New Slav., and Serbian.

In the Serbian language only does this word, whence is taken the Greek *vrykolakas*, mean rather a vampire than a werewolf. It is probable that this is to be explained by the fact that it is generally held among all Slavonic peoples that the man who has during his life been a werewolf almost necessarily becomes a vampire after his death. None the less a vampire need not once have been a werewolf, and the two must be most carefully distinguished. They are entirely different, separate, and apart.

The Slavonic word for vampire is that which we have taken over in English, *vampirŭ*. I will again quote Miklosich[69]: "Vampirŭ: b. vampir, vapir, vepir, vЪpir, *wampir. Davon* vepirêsvam se, vampirêsvam se. *s.* vampir. *p.* upior, upierzyca *neben* wampir. *kh.* vampyr, vepyr, vopyr, opyr, vpyr, opir, *neben* uper. upýr, upyrjaka *für r.* urodЪ, urodyšče. *wr.* upir, chodjaščij mertvec, kror čelovêču pЪeć. *r.* upirt (klali trêbu upiremiЪ), upyrЪ, obyrЪ *neben* vampiriЪ *ein gespenst, das den menschen das blut aussaugt. Im s. und r. ist der vukodlak werwolf und der wampir in eins verschmolzen. Das wort ist wahrscheinlich türk.: nordtürk,* ube.r *hexe, nsl.* vêdomec, prêmrl (*erstarrt*)."

A vampire, then, is altogether another thing from a werewolf. The former is dead; the latter is fearfully alive, although there has been much confusion and there is indeed a connection of a sort between the two. Moreover, Mr. J. C. Lawson points out that "there is evidence that in the Greek language itself the word *vrykolakas* does even now locally and occasionally bear its original significance".[70] Curiously enough, an eminent authority denies this, for Bernhard Schmidt in his discussion of the term βρυκόλακας and its many variants writes: "Allein das Wort ist unzweifelhaft slavischen Ursprungs und identisch mit dem

23

slavischen Namen des Werwolfs, welcher böhmisch vlkodlak, bulgarisch und slovakisch vrkolak (für vrkodlak), polnisch, vilkolak oder vilkolek lautet, was wörtlich 'Wolfshaar, Wolfspelz' heisst, indem serb. dlaka und altböhm. tlak Haare bedeutet. Nun sind zwar Werwolf und Vampyr im Grunde ganz verschiedene Wesen, indem man unter jenem einem lebendigen Menschen versteht, der sich zu Zeiten in einer alles zerfleischenden Wolf verwandelt, unter diesem dagegen einen verstorbenen, der aus seinem Grabe wieder kommt und den Lebenden durch Aussaugen ihres Blutes den Untergang bereitet; und der neugriechische βουρκόλακας entspricht nur dem letzteren. Da indessen doch beide blutgierige, auf Menschenmord ausgehende Geschöpfe sind, und der Vampyr auch seinerseits, gleich dem Werwolf, Thiergestalt anzunehmen vermag, so konnten sie in der Vorstellung des Volkes leicht mit einander vermengt werden und demzu folge der Name des einen auf den Begriff des anderen übergehen Wirklich lässt sich dieser Vorgang bei slavischen Stämmen sicher nachweisen, z. B. den Serben, in deren Sprache vukodlak den Vampyr bezeichnet. Hier durch wird die Slavicität des Namens βουρκόλακας über jeden Zweifel gehoben."[71]

Schmidt's somewhat dogmatic pronouncement is, however, clearly and demonstrably erroneous, nor does he help his case by seeking to dismiss at least two pieces of incontrovertible evidence in a footnote.[72] He has, indeed, fallen into the fatal error of wresting or rather of attempting to wrest facts to fit his preconceived theories. Hanush[73] was informed by a Greek of Mytilene that there were two distinct kinds of *vrykolakes*, the one sort being men already dead (the vampire), the other living men who were subject to a weird somnambulism which sent them forth ravening, and this particularly on moonlight nights. (Cf. Gervase of Tilbury's "Vidimus enim frequenter in Anglia *per lunationes* homines in lupos mutari".)[74] Again, Cyprian Robert in his *Les Slaves de Turquie*,[75] thus describes the *vrykolakes* of Thessaly and Epirus: "Ce sont des hommes vivants en proie à une sorte de somnambulisme, qui, saisis par la soif du carnage, sortent la nuit de leurs huttes de bergers, et courent la campagne, déchirant de leurs morsures tout ce qu'ils rencontrent, hommes on bestiaux." Here, too, the connection between shepherds and the werewolves is striking. Amongst other shepherds who were proved to be addicted to werewolfery there is the notorious case of Pierre Burgot and Michel Verdun, a couple of lycanthropic sorcerers who were tried at Besançon in December, 1521, and sentenced to be burned alive by the Inquisitor General, Frère Jean Boin, O.P.[76]

Mr. J. C. Lawson also brings forward new evidence[77] and such as, in spite of Schmidt's contradictions, puts the matter beyond all doubt that the *vrykolakas* is a werewolf. He relates how in Cyprus whilst excavations were being carried out under the auspices of the British Museum during the spring of 1899, the directors heard from their workmen several stories concerning the detection of *vrykolakes*. In one particular village the inhabitants having suffered terribly from the depredations of a nocturnal marauder, armed themselves and kept a strick look out for the evil scourge. Before long in the moonlight watches they espied a *vrykolakas*, and one of the company either with gun or sword succeeded in wounding the monster, who, however, escaped and fled away into the shadows. The next day it was observed that a certain man in the village, who had not been among the picket, was marked with a wound exactly corresponding to the hurt inflicted on the *vrykolakas* the night before. When he was nearly interrogated the varlet at length confessed that he was indeed a *vrykolakas* and the nocturnal visitant of ill.

Mr. Lawson tells how he was informed by peasants on the borders of Aetolia and Acarnania, in the neighbourhood of Agrinion, that the word *vrykolakas* is occasionally applied to living persons in the sense of werewolf, although it is true to say the more common use may be the general "vampire".

I myself can add a quota of evidence, as during my travels in Greece I heard the word *vrykolakas* employed by a peasant to describe a man strongly suspect of sorcery who, as it was firmly believed, wandered abroad at night for purposes of rapine and ravishment, and who had woefully assaulted individuals and torn out the throats of flocks. Whether this wretch assumed or was seen in the shape of a wolf I could not exactly learn.

Incidentally it may be remarked that the explanations given by Hépitès in his *Lexicon*[78] under βρυκόλακας are a little superficial, not to say incorrect: "βρυκόλακας, καὶ βουρκόλακας. ψυχὴ περιπλανωμένη εἰς τὴν γῆν. ψυχῆς σκινειδὲς Οαντασμα, *revenant*, n.m. brucolaque, n.m. Οάντασμα αἱμοδιψές, vampire, n.f. ἡ ἔμπουσα."

"βρυκολακιάζω, μέλ. άσω. ἐπανέρχομαι μετὰ τὸν θάνατον εἰς τὴν γῆν ὡς βροκόλακας (ὡς πνεῦμα, Οάντασμα) *revenir comme esprit* (ἢ *comme revenant*); || αὐτὸ τὸ σπίτι εἶνε βρυκολακιασμένον, *il revient dans cette maison; cette maison est hantée*; (στοιχειωμένος, η, ον. ὁ συχναζόμενος ὑπὸ Οαντασμάτων)• βλ• καὶ στοιχειώνω• || λέγουν ὅτι ἐβρυκολάκιασεν ἀΟοῦ ἀπέθανε, *on dit qu'il revenait après sa mort.*" "βρυκόλαξ, ακος. ὁ. βλ. βρυκόλακας."

The Latin word for a werewolf was *versipellis* (*verto-pellis*), the original adjective having the meaning "that changes its skin" and hence in general "that changes its shape or form". So in the *Amphitruo*[79] Plautus makes Mercury, who speaks the Prologue, say of Jupiter, who has turned himself into the very guise and exact counterpart of Amphitryon—

ita versipellem se facit quando lubet.

Pliny in the *Historia Naturalis*, VIII, xxii, "De lupis," drily comments upon the werewolf legends of Greece, "homines in lupos verti, rursumque restitui sibi, falsum esse confidenter existimare debemus, aut credere omnia, quae fabulosa tot saeculis comperimus. Unde tamen ista vulgo infixa sit fama in tantum, ut in maledictis versipelles habeat, indicabitur." In the most famous werewolf story of antiquity, perhaps of all time, told by the freedman Niceros at the table of Trimalchio, the narrator relates how to his abject horror he saw the young soldier transform himself into a wolf, and when the animal was wounded in the neck, later the man was found to have an ugly gash just in the same spot. "Intellexi ilium versipellem esse, nec postea cum illo panem gustare potui, non si me occidisses." ("Then I realized that he was a werewolf in full sooth, and I couldn't have eaten a mouthful with him, no, not if you had killed me outright.")[80] Apuleius uses the word *versipellis* of the transformation of witches into any animal or insect, birds, dogs, mice, flies, "cum deterrimae versipelles in quodvis animal ore converso adrepant, ut ipsos etiam oculos Solis et Iustitiae facile frusterentur."[81]

In the history of *Barlaam and Josaphat*, formerly ascribed to S. Gregory Nanzianzen,[82] c. xxx, the phrase καὶ γνοὺς τὰ μηχανήματα τοῦ δολίου Jacques de Billy[83] turns by "intellectisque *uersipellis* hostis technis atque artibus",[84] and a little later in the same chapter for ταῦτα συλλαλήσας ὁ δολιόΟρων τοῖς ἑαυτοῦ κυσὶν he has: "haec cum *versipellis* ille ad socios dixisset."[85] Hence we see *versipellis* aptly applied as a name for the demon.

Not impertinently then does Julius Briêger in his *Flores Caluinistici* describe Robert Dudley, Earl of Leicester, as *Versipellis*. Relating the efforts of this villain to urge Queen Elizabeth against the Blessed Thomas Howard, Duke of Norfolk, he writes: "*Ille vero* (ut Versipellisest) *Reginam in Ducē concitare hac conatur ratione.*"[86]

Later authors almost invariably express the werewolf and werewolfery by a periphrasis, as for example, "Credidisti . . . ut quandocunque ille homo voluerit, in lupum transformari possit, quod teutonice Werewulf vocatur?" of the Burchard *Penetential* (c. 1000); "homines substantialiter in lupos non sunt conversi, sed, . . . lupi apparent," of Peter Mamor, who wrote about 1462, in his *Flagellum maleficorum*[87]; and Weyer's "lupi noxii, quos lamias putant, Germanis *Werwolff* dicti".[88]

In later medical writers "lycanthropia", often in Greek characters, appears signifying the disease, and "lycanthropus" denotes the sufferer. But "lycanthropus" is never employed to mean a werewolf, in which sense Du Cange does not recognize this word, although under *lupus* he has: "*Loup beroux*, idem qui *Loup-garou* vulgatius appellatur, in Lit. remiss. ann. 1415 ex Reg. 169. Charloph. reg. ch. 204: *Ribault prestre, champiz, Loup beroux, etc.* Haud scio an eadem acceptione *Leu wasté* legitur in aliis Lit. ann. 1355. ex Reg. 84. ch. 65: *Quamplurima verba injuriosa de dictis Johanne et ejus uxore dixit Johannes Cosset, et specialiter dictum Johannem vocarit Leu wasté et ejus uxorem ribaude.*"[89] Thus in the fourteenth century we have "werewolf" used as a term of abuse, and so foul and slanderous in its application that the name was violently resented.

Neither Forcellini[90] nor Maigne d'Arnis[91] include "lycanthropus", and the term is evidently regarded as wholly Greek. It is uncertain, indeed, whether the word is to be found with the meaning "werewolf" before the seventeenth century, when it occurs in a marginal gloss, "*exemplum de Lycanthropo*," on part i, question x, of the *Malleus Maleficarum* in the quarto edition of 1669,[92] vol. i, p. 67.

It is amply evident from the etymological history of the word "werewolf" with its many cognates and equivalents in every European language, that the tradition is not only most anciently and universally diffused throughout the whole of this great continent, but that it has further indelibly impressed itself upon the common speech and struck deep into the imagination of the Western peoples. Nor is it merely a grim superstition; it is a terrible and dangerous truth, and one, moreover, which is by no means confined to Europe alone. A serious belief in some metamorphosis or transformation may be found over the whole wide world. It is not necessarily a change into the wolf, for there are records in other countries of shape-shifting to a very wide variety of animals. In Northern Europe the shape thus assumed was called *hamr*; the process of changing *at skipta hömum* or *at hamz*; the travelling in such a form *hamfarir*; and the supernatural strength acquired by such metamorphosis *hamremmi*. But it must be carefully borne in mind that the soul remains unchanged, and that therefore the eye, which is the mirror of the soul, is also unchanged. In Scandinavian lore no animal is more highly esteemed than the Bear. He is considered rational, and in the Finnbogi saga Finnbogi converses with him, calling him *bessi*. Among the most famous *hamrammir* were the *berserkir*, the bearmen, or were-bears. (Their skin is called *bjarnahamr*, and they have the enormous strength of a bear, which state, however, alternates with extreme lassitude.) Among the gods and heroes of Norse legend transformations are common. They are often effected by putting on the skins of beasts or fur and feather mantles. The goddesses Frigg and Freyja have their "falcon-cloaks" *valshamr*; the Valkyries their *alptar hamir* "swan-cloaks", and *krakuhamir* "ravencloaks".[93]

In modern Greece the transformation into a boar, the were-boar, ἀγριογούρουνο, is believed.[94] The Wallachians dread the *priccolitsh*, the weredog.[95]

In Abyssinia and in the Egyptian Soudan the wizards are credited with the power of becoming hyenas at will.[96] Throughout that vast continent man metamorphoses himself into many other animals, the leopard, the jaguar, the lion, the elephant, the crocodile, the alligator, and even into fish such as the shark.[97]

Throughout India, but more particularly in the northern Himalayan districts, the weretiger prowls; in Java, Borneo, and the Malay States there are wereleopards to boot.[98] The weretiger is also known in China and Japan, but here the werefox is both feared and honoured. The werebadger and the weredog are also sorcerers, sometimes it may be friendly sorcerers, in animal shape.[99]

The Toradjas of the Central Celebes give their wizards a yet wider range of metamorphosis which includes cats, crocodiles, wild pigs, apes, deer, and buffaloes.[100] In the West Indies we return to the transformation into a hyena.[101] In North America we meet once more the werewolf as also the werebuffalo.[102]

Of old in Central America, in Mexico and Peru, men knew

the weretiger, the were-eagle, and the wereserpent.[103] In South America generally to-day the warlock is generally credited to shift his shape to the jaguar, but there are also tales of weretigers, were-eagles, and wereserpents.[104] The witches of Chili are credited with the power of turning themselves into a chonchon, a bird resembling a vulture which flies by night, whilst others assume the appearance of the calchona, described as a beast with long grey hair, something between a goat and a prairie dog.[105]

In order then to satisfy his lust for blood, his desire to hurt, harm, and kill, to terrify and amaze, the witch, the bond-slave of Satan, by his master's evil power and hellish craft transforms or seems to transform himself into the shape of some ravening beast of prey, and naturally enough this animal will be that most commonly met with in the district where the varlet inhabits. This explains clearly enough and logically enough why the werewolf is rare to-day, why "there can nowhere be a living belief in contemporary metamorphosis into any animal which has ceased to exist in the particular locality".[106] For long centuries throughout all Europe there was no wilder brute, no more dreaded enemy of man than the savage wolf, whose ferocity was a quick and lively menace to the countryside such as perhaps we cannot in these later days by any stretch of imagination even faintly realize and apprehend. Whilst yet large tracts of every country, steppes and moorland, sierra and wold, upland, fell and plain, were utterly deserted and only trodden by man with peril and mortal danger to himself, the wolf proved a fearful foe. He dwelt in the heart of those impenetrable forests which long continued his veritable strongholds, fortresses whence he could not be dislodged, Riddlesdale and Bowland, Sherwood and Bere and Irwell in England; Ettrick, Braemar, Rothiemurchus, Invercauld in Scotland; in Ireland Kilmallock, the wilds of Kerry, the Wicklow mountains, Shillela; in France, Fontainebleau, Vincennes, the thick-hedged slopes of the Jura and Vosges; in Germany and central Europe the Schwarzwald, the Böhmerwald, Wald-Viertel, and many more. Monarchs hunted him, and legislated and offered rich rewards for his destruction. But for many a hundred years and hundred years again did the wolf defy all attempts at extirpation. What better guise, what better shape of fear and ferocity could the shape-shifting sorcerer in Europe assume?

The werewolf is the main object of our study; the werewolf who is metamorphosed by black magic, by occult and most hideous bedevilment.

"Lycanthropy or Wolf-madness, a Variety of Isania Zoanthropica"[107] is, says a recent authority, "endemic insanity."[108] *Daemonium lupinum* was the recognized name for this disease, as Bernard Gordonius testifies.[109]

It is now quite generally recognized that insanity is very frequently nothing else than diabolical possession. Heurnius (Jan van Hewin), *De Mania, De Morbis Capitis*, c. xiii, says: "Profecto non sine daemone saepe haec calamitas. Permissu summi Dei illi spiritus sensibus incomperti se corporibus insinuant, receptique visceribus valetudinem bonam vastant: somnia terrent, ac formidine animam quatiunt."[110] It were superfluous here once again to demonstrate the facts of possession, "which is one of the most articulately expressed doctrines of both Testaments, and which reigned for seventeen hundred years, hardly challenged, in all the churches."[111] The express witness of Our Divine Lord Himself, both in word and deed, cannot be gainsaid, and is, of course, final and complete.[112] The disease lycanthropy, then, is in the majority of cases, perhaps in all, demoniacal possession.

It is true that the physicians nicely distinguish two kinds of lycanthropy; the one arising from possession by the Devil, the other natural, as Daniel Sennert[113] says. At which point it is necessary to emphasize very explicitly the difference between lycanthropy and werwolfery, since these are two diverse and heterogeneous things, although both are clearly of a Satanic origin. (An exception may possibly be made if there is adduced so as to convince us an instance of "natural lycanthropy", although I hold that such can hardly be.) The sufferer, the lycanthrope, may, it is true, be an innocent victim, thus woefully afflicted "that the works of God should be made manifest in him",[114] as was the man who was blind from his birth, and whom Our Lord healed. Often, again, it is that Satan has betrayed his servant the sorcerer, the werewolf, has plagued him and driven him mad to make him more miserable in life and to involve him even more irretrievably in perdition, for the sorcerer is one who has made a pact with the Devil, and, as Guazzo points out, these pacts "are not only vain and useless; they are also dangerous and immeasurably pernicious".[115] Remy also speaks of all who have surrendered themselves to the power of the Demon, as weary of his tyranny and bitterly conscious of their guilt, ever wishing to throw off the yoke of evil, so harsh and unjust a taskmaster is Satan,[116] who chides and punishes them sorely at each motion towards good, each inspiration of grace.

We have just spoken of those who are innocent victims of evil, and lest there be some misunderstanding or ambiguity with regard to this particular point, one which has already confessedly offered difficulties and (I fear) led some into error, it will accordingly not merely be fitting but also incumbent to inquire how far and in what manner by the aid of the Devil witches are able to torment and torture others, to harm and waste men's goods, to visit their bodies with sickness, even to kill and bring to the grave.

The subject has been discussed at ample length and in all its bearings by authorities of the first order, by Kramer and Sprenger in the *Malleus Maleficarum*, by Bishop Binsfeld and Bodin, by Guazzo, Remy, Paulus Grillandus, Delrio, Jacques d'Autun, and many more, but since we are in some sort dealing with it particularly as it regards or may regard lycanthropy we will consider quite briefly the quiddity of the whole question, whether in fact witches and sorcerers can and do afflict others by their spells, charms, and cantrips, their periapts and fascinations, as it is debated by a learned physician, the eminent Daniel Sennert, in the ninth part of his *De Morbis Occultis*,[117] and although we are indeed unable to agree with him on many points he never strays *contra fidem,* and correcting his erroneous propositions from more orthodox and sounder treatises we can profit not a little from the general arguments he advances with such skill and learning.

Born at Breslau on 25th November, 1572, Daniel Sennert was early distinguished by his great parts and his intense application to study. He lectured *summa cum laude* at Wittenburg, and although there were indeed those who said that so vast was his library learning he excelled more in the theoretic rather than in the practic, none the less he was in 1628 appointed body physician to George I, Elector of Saxony. Sennert died of the plague at Wittenburg on 21st July, 1637, being 65 years old. One of his most famous works is the *Practica Medicina,* published 4to 1628.[118]

Much dialectic and controversy, a good deal of misconception and inexactitude, might have been saved had certain writers who took upon themselves to assail the results and reports of experience and reason but borne carefully in mind that these mischiefs cannot be wrought by the Demon at the instigation of his slaves and devotees were they not allowed and permitted by the power of Almighty God—*Deo permittente* is the vital clause. The chief source of error seems to have lain in some notion that the evidence of the Devil's handiwork and his interference with the affairs of men to their hurt and bane seems to impugn the Omnipotence of God. As the Capuchin Jacques d'Autun lays down: "*Sola permissio Dei est causa cur Dœmon possideat corpus.*" He adds: "Quoy? la diuine Prouidence abandōnera les iustes à la malice & à la rage d'vn Magicien esclaue du Demon: Et Dieu qui à donné des Anges Gardiens pour la conseruation des Creatures rachetées de son Sang, les abandonnera à la furie d'vne Megere? Des opinions si mal fondées, ne sont receuës que du Vulgaire, que ne sçait pas que les Magiciens, ny toutes les puissances de l'Enfer ne peuuent rien attenter sur vne personne consacrée à Dieu par le Baptesme, *si Dieu ne le permet*; que s'il y a des Possedez (comme il n'y a nul doute) les malefices des Sorciers n'en font pas la cause, il faut rapporter vne si rude épreuue en des foibles Creatures, *à la seule permission Diuine.* Le Concile d'Ephese d'où cette verité est tirée, ne reconnoit point d'autre cause, & les Theologiens qui l'ont regardé comme vn phase, pour éuiter de semblables écueils, ont rapporté la possession des Demons, non à la malice des Esprits rebelles, ny aux charmes & Sortileges des Magiciens ou Sorciers, mais à la permission Diuine."[119] The Fathers continually remind us how the demons fear and tremble exceedingly before God, as, for example, S. Cyril of Alexandria, who in his magnificent *Encomium in sanctam Mariam Deiparam*, addressing himself to Nestorius, writes: Ἀλλ' οὐ πιστεύεις προφήταις καὶ ἀποστόλοις, καὶ εὐαγγελισταῖς καὶ τῷ ἀρχαγγέλῳ Γαβριήλ; κἂν τοὺς συν δαίμονάς σου μίμησαι, τοὺς Ὁρίξαντας αὐτοῦ τὴν δύναμιν καὶ Οωνήσαντας. "Τί ἡμῖν καὶ σοὶ Ἰησοῦ Υἱὲ τοῦ Θεοῦ; Ἦλθες ὧδε πρὸ καιροῦ βασανίσαι ἡμᾶς."[120]

As King James has so very pertinently and convincingly written: "For since by God's permission, he [the Devil] layed sicknesse vpon IOB, why may he not farre easilier lay it vpon any other. For as an old practisian, he knows well inough what humor domines most in anie of vs, and as a spirite hee can subtillie waeken vp the same, making it peccant, or to abounde, as he thinkes meete for troubling of vs, when God will so permit him."[121]

Not only indeed have we in Scripture the example of holy Job whom God permitted Satan to plague with the loss of all his possessions, the deaths of his children, and "a very grievous ulcer, from the sole of the foot even to the top of his head", but we are expressly told: "There are spirits that are created for vengance, and in their fury they lay on grievous torments."[122]

Dr. Daniel Sennert inquires whether diseases can be brought upon a man by means of spells and black magic, so that such a one will wither, consume and decay, peak and pine, and even fall away into death. It is universally agreed that if such an evil charm can prevail it will be wrought in one (or more) of three ways: firstly, by a look, a malign glance, the evil eye; secondly, by the voice, the mutter of some occult rune, and especially by presumptuously overpraising and in scorn extolling him to be harmed[123]; thirdly, by a touch, a contact, exsufflation or gesture.[124]

Sennert does not, however, discuss a point which we may pause to ask. Have these charms, these cantrips, this abacadabra, and these sigils any evil influence in themselves, and if not why then are they employed by sorcerers and witches when about their foul businesses?

Let Jacques d'Autun answer our first question: "Il est vray que les Sorciers par leurs paroles & ceremonies superstitieuses, ne contribuënt pas à l'effet du malefice. I'ay desja dit que leurs mots barbares sont sans vertu, & que de tous les maux qu'il pretendent faire, le Demon en est l'Autheur; mais il ne le feroit pas, si le Sorcier n'estoit de concert auecque luy, & si non seulement il ne donnoit son consentement, mais encore s'il ne preparoit les sorts & les charmes, auecque les circonstances dont ils ont conuenu. I'auoüe qu'ils sont les instruments du Demon, lequel à la veuë des signes de leur Paction, execute le mal qu'il leur a promis de faire; mais ce ne sont pas que des Instruments in animez."[125] Accordingly we may be well assured that these mutterings and incantations, these secret songs and signs, have of themselves no power to effect the desired end. That is wrought by the Devil with the co-operation of the will of the witch, who prays and urges him to accomplish the evil act, the blighting of crops, the smiting of cattle with murrain or man with sickness, whatever the intention may be. Yet these words and gestures have a very deep and vital significance not *per se* but *per accidens*. They are the symbols and witnesses of the unholy pact between Satan and the sorcerer, and blasphemy moreover possesses of itself a compelling attraction for evil spirits, so that in a very real sense the fiend, urged and reminded by these evocations, performs his part of the contract and will inevitably demand (although not in right nor in justice) that the other conditions also be fulfilled at the appointed time. Moreover, Satan in his boundless pride is always first and foremost desirous of homage and worship, that adoration due to God alone. The last, and as it were the climax, of Our Lord's three temptations was the mysterious view of "all the kingdoms of the world, and the glory of them" with the Devil's whispered words: "All these will I give thee, if falling down thou wilt adore me."[126] Therein Satan put forth the exercise of all his strength and unveiled his ultimate purpose. Now the witch by these spells and charms, which are the medial (but not essential) instrumentality of working evil, definitely pays that homage to the powers of evil which the demon craves and demands. Therefore by no means must they be omitted or forborne.

Having made clear this important circumstance we return to the treatise of Sennert. Many authors are quoted in the *De Morbis Occultis*, historians, physicians, philosophers, and poets: Vergil, Plato, Ovid, Cicero, Pliny, Plutarch, Vida, Aristotle, Galen, Livy, Suetonius, Heliodorus, Apuleius, Hippocrates, Weyer, Boece, Scaliger, Nicolas Jacquerius, Cardan, Cornelius Gemma, Antonio Beneveni, Bodin, Remy, Alessandro Benedicti, Gregory Horstius, Battista Codronchi, John Languis, Zacuto of Lisbon, and other names of lesser note.

In the first place Sennert is demonstrably in error when he writes that in his opinion warlocks and evil folk cannot injure others by a look, and he inclines to reduce any ill results which follow from overlooking to the effects of imagination aggravated by terror and alarm, so that those weak subjects who are prone to an epilepsy or hysterical affections might indeed fall ill after but not owing to the malignant glance of some reputed witch. Setting aside the possibilities and powers of hypnotism, and the horrible influence of the evil eye which cannot be gainsaid, since there are the famous cases of the *eye-biting* witches of Ireland[127]; and S. Thomas lays down that the eye is able to work evil on an external object, so that when a soul is vehemently moved to wickedness, as occurs mostly in little old women, the countenance becomes venemous and hurtful wherein spiteful demons co-operate, whilst in the *Malleus Maleficarum* it is definitely stated that there are witches who can bewitch "by a mere look or glance from their eyes", so that as Blessed Angelo says the evil eye is a matter of common knowledge and daily experience.[128]

Beliefs and practices relating to the evil eye, all extremely similar in nature, are found the whole world over from the earliest times.[129] Thus this fascination is spoken of in the Vedas,[130] the Zendavesta,[131] whilst allusions are not infrequent in Greek and Latin literature.[132] It occurs with the Slavs,[133] the Scandinavians,[134] and among Celtic peoples. The Etruscans and the ancient Egyptians feared the bale of the evil eye.[135] In Assyrian incantations it is guarded against,[136] whilst the Jewish,[137] Phœnician,[138] and Carthaginian traditions have influenced the creed of Mohammed.[139] In Scotland[140] and in modern Greece[141]; in England, particularly in the northern and more westerly counties[142]; in Morocco[143] and North Africa[144]; in Central Africa[145] and among the Zulus[146]; among the Bushmen[147]; in Asia with the Chinese and Tibetans[148]; in the Malay Archipelago[149] and in Polynesia[150]; among the peoples of America, North, Central, and Southern[151]; everywhere men dread and have always dreaded the glance of the evil eye.[152]

Bacon said in his essay *Of Enuy*, that both Love and Envy "come easily into the Eye, especially vpon the presence of the Obiects; which are the Points, that conduce to Fascination, if any such thing there be. We see likewise, the Scripture calleth *Enuy*, An *Euill Eye*: And the Astrologers, call the euill Influences of the Starrs, *Euill Aspects*; So that still, there seemeth to be acknowledged, in the Act of *Enuy*, an Eiaculation, or Irradiation of the Eye". He further remarks: "the Act of Enuy, had somewhat in it, of *Witchcraft*; so there is no other Cure of *Enuy*, but the Cure of *Witchcraft*: And that is, to remoue the *Lot* (as they call it) and to lay it vpon another."[153] Leonard Vair in his *De Fascino*, speaking of the eyes as "alter animus", writes: "Ex ipsis radii quidam emittuntur, qui veluti iacula quaedam, ac sagittae ad effascinandorum corda deferuntur, totumque corpus inficiunt, atque ita nulla interposita mora arbores, segetes, bruta animalia, et homines perniciosa qualitate inficiunt, et ad interitum deducunt." It is not without significance that Mr. J. C. Lawson remarked: "The evil eye, it would seem, is a regular attribute both of the Gorgon and of the wolf." Experience indeed will not permit us to doubt that there are to-day no few yelder-eyed witches.

Sennert then catalogues and discusses the various names given to sorcerers and witches: they are *pharmaceutriae, incantatores, veneficae, maleficae, magi, sagae, lamiae, striges,* and their craft is *ars atracia,* "die Schroarkefunst," "non quidem ab atro colore sed ab Atrace in Thessalia."[154]However these several kinds of witches may slightly differ one from another, some using one sort of spoken spell and some another, a philtre or brew, they all have this in common, they have made a pact with the Devil of which the chief article is the renunciation of God, and the chief intent to ensue evil and do it.

Especially do they raise strife in households, they sow discord betwixt man and wife,[155] they procure sterility and abortion, and strike man in his deepest affections, in human love, depriving him of the virile member, "membrum virile veneficio ablatum."[156] These acts are particularly reprobated in the famous Bull of Innocent VIII, *Summis desiderantes affectibus,* 9th December, 1484.[157] Sennert indeed quotes from Condrochi, whose authority he was apparently unaware is the *Malleus Maleficarum.*[158] He also has an interesting history from Zacuto, under whose direct notice the incidents came. A young gallant of Lisbon endeavouring to gain the love of a maiden aged 16, the child of worthy and wealthy parents, had recourse to a witch. This hag moulded a wax image of the girl and used various incantations, with the result that the victim fell into an extraordinary sickness that baffled the physicians, who deemed she was suffering from some affection of the womb. Wellnigh at their wits' end, her parents secretly consulted an astrologer, and eventually the girl was cured by the help of a sorceress. Before she was finally freed she vomited a creature like a mouse.[159]

Sennert controverts and refutes Weyer, whose opinion was

that diseases cannot be induced by spells. He points out that the Devil is most skilled in poisons, that he instructs his servants in the art of venefices, and in many cases no doubt they bring about the illness owing to the subtle introduction of some toxicant. Some diseases which are natural they heighten and aggravate; others they induce by their powders and unguents. The Devil can afflict men as he afflicted with God's permission Holy Job,[160] but when he torments men this is not owing to the power of the witch, although she is deceived and thinks the ill is due to her. The Devil works on natural causes to produce disease. He also procures sterility and abortion. He can also hurt and harm men by sudden violence. He mocks his slaves by glamour and illusion.

Although the evil is not done by the power of the witches, they are none the less equally guilty. Upon this point, we may remark, all authorities are agreed, and it will suffice to quote Jacques d'Autun, who sums up the matter very clearly and concisely by emphasizing that the essential crime of the sorcerer lies in the fact he has worshipped the Devil, giving Satan that honour and glory which belong to the Majesty of God alone: "c'est pour cette raison, que quand mesme le Sorcier n'auroit commis aucun Crime, dont le prochain auroit esté endommagé, il meriteroit la mort comme coupable du crime de leze-Majesté Diuine, & Humaine, commis contre la personne de IESVS-CHRIST, Dieu & homme."[161]

Sennert reviews the arguments of Weyer, which upon examination he dismisses as trite and useless. He then remarks that pacts with Satan are essentially "mendacia et fallacia". "Fallit Diabolus." "Licet magna Diaboli sit potestas nulli tamen etiam ad sagarum voluntatem nocere potest sine Dei permissione."

The various cures for a disease of diabolic origin are listed and commented upon,[162] whence rises the point whether a sufferer may apply to a witch to relieve the sickness which has been induced by a witch. Sennert replies: No, it is not lawful. This, however, remains a very difficult and dubious question,[163] and although Sennert is so definite in his negative, the conclusion is not quite so easy. The Venerable Duns Scotus, Blessed Henry of Segusio, Godfrey of Fontaines, Ubertino of Casale, Francesco Maria Guazzo,[164] and other authorities not a few argue that it is permissible to remove witchcraft even by superstitious and vain means, since it is meritorious to destroy the works of the Devil, which indeed is hardly to be disputed. On the other hand, S. Thomas, S. Bonaventura, S. Albertus Magnus, Peter a Palude, Boguet,[165] and other great names maintain a contrary opinion.

Fra José Angles, a Franciscan of Valencia, titular bishop of Posonium, who is regarded as a theologian of moderate and equable views, in his *Flores Theologicarum Quaestionum in II. Sent.*, Madriti, 1586, Quaestio unica *De Arte Magica*,[166] Artie, vi. "An liceat sine peccato opera diaboli uti"; Secunda diffic., "Utrum liceat uti opera eius, qui maleficia exercet?"[167] asks whether it is permissible to request or persuade a man to unlock, dissolve, or impede a spell, if there is none the less good reason to believe such relief cannot be effected without the mediation of the demon or the confection of some further spell? He decides that it is not lawful, inasmuch as the wizard cannot perform the operation without recourse to the aid of Satan, which is in itself a heinous sin, and he who requests or induces another to commit a sin himself becomes the partaker of and participator in that sin. Bishop Angles will not even allow a man "bona fide magicis incantationibus et adjurationibus uti".[168] But here the whole point turns on *magicis* and *adjurationibus*. Assuredly we must not consent to nor yet take part, however remotely, in any magical practices or casting of spells. But it is the direct opposite of consenting to a thing if we destroy that thing. A spell may not then be counter-checked by another spell, but it may be dissolved by burning the instrument of evil.

Yet that great and grave theologian Blessed Angelo Carletti di Chivasso (1411–1495), in his *Summa de Casibus Conscientiæ* (the *Summa Angelica*),[169] under the title *Superstitio*, 18, relying upon the *Doctor Facundus*, Pietro Aureoli,[170] whom John XXII appointed Archbishop of Aix in 1321, and referring to his

Commentarium in Sententiarum IV (iv distinctio, xxxiv, quaest.
2), permits a man in order that a spell may be removed to have
recourse to or consult with one ever defamed as witch. These two
Franciscan theologians base their judgment upon S. Augustine,
who in the matter of an oath laid down "licitum mihi esse uti ad
commodum meum juramento hominis infidelis quamvis sciam
illum juraturum per Deos suos falsos quos colit".[171]

It were superfluous to emphasize that neither Pietro Aureoli
nor Blessed Angelo tolerate any dealing with the demon. It is
argued that it does not follow that because a witch has learned
her art from an evil source, every exercise of that art or every
result of that art must necessarily be evil.

Blessed Angelo writes: "Utrum sciens maleficium possit sine
periculo illud solvere. Secundum Petrum Aureolum [*l.c.*], aliud
maleficium fieri non potest sine peccato infidelitatis." He then
quotes S. Augustine: "de juramento infidelis jurantis in nomine
dei sui." "Non possit inducere aliquem ad aliquid maleficium
faciendum. Si tunc est aliquis dispositio actualiter facere aliquid
maleficium ut aliquid destruat possum illo uti ad bonum meum.
potest etiam tolli per destructionem maleficii sui sciens quia
eo destructo demon non amplius fatigaret, quia ex pacto non
assistit nisique diu durat tale signum. [Ven. Dun Scotus is then
cited.] Nedum non est peccatum: immo meritorium destruere
opera diaboli. Nec in hoc est infidelitas aliqua, quia destructio
non ad quies cit operibus diaboli, sed credit demonem posse
vexare et velle fatigare dum tale signum durat. Et destructio
signi talis imponit finem vexationis. Potest etiam destruere
quis maleficia per sacrata: adjurationes divitias: orationes et
hujusmodi meritoria."[172]

Alfonso de Castro in his *De Iusta Haereticorum Punitione*,
Libri iii (Lugduni, 1556), i, 15,[173] lays down that it is not permissible
to dissolve one spell by working another spell. He terms it justly
"malum pessimum" to seem to give countenance to any operation
which may involve the invocation or the reliance upon the help
of a familiar. He teaches, in fine, that "maleficium solicitans,

ut maleficium maleficio solvat, graviter peccat". But, and here we really have the important point, he concludes: "Si autem maleficium tale esset ut sine peccato posset a malefico dissolvi, ut puta, quia scit ubi laqueus aut imago, aut ligaturae aliquae, aut characteres cum quibus est jam inceptum maleficium, tune sicut ipse potest sine peccato dissolvere maleficium confringendo illa omnia, ita quilibet alius potest sine peccato petere ab ipso malefico, ut illo modo dissolvat maleficium."[174]

The whole matter is considered at some length by Kramer and Sprenger, who acknowledge that here we have a most nice dilemma. They conclude that we must distinguish the various classes and kinds of remedies. There are, in fine, three general conditions whereby any remedy is, in ordinary circumstances, rendered unlawful. First, when the spell is removed through the agency of another witch, and by further witchcraft, that is to say, by some evil power. Secondly, when the spell is removed not by a witch but by an honest person in such a way, however, that it is placed upon another individual. Thirdly, when the spell is removed by an honest person and not even placed upon another, but when some open or tacit invocation of devils or operation of black magic is employed in the process. At the same time there are remedies which, if they do not injure another person, may be tolerated even should they smack somewhat of superstitious usage and vanity. Further details can be read in the *Malleus Maleficarum*, part ii, question 2, introduction,[175] to which reference should be made.

"Maleficia maleficiis curare non licet," definitely pronounces the Bishop of Benevento, Giovanni Francesco Leone, in his *Libellus de Sortilegiis*, c. xii; for he adds: "Mala enim non sunt facienda, ut eveniant bona: maleficiorum curatio a Deo est impetranda, qui omnia potest," wise words of infinite consolation and encouragement.[176]

Further, Sennert asks: *An liceat instrumenta Magica quaerere et abolere?*[177] Curiously enough he adopts an extraordinary position, and now contends at great length that it is not lawful to seek out, discover, and burn such instruments or implements of witchdom as are the media of conveying harm. For, he says, that by destroying such and looking for a good result as the consequence of their demolition, one is in some sense acknowledging the Devil's power. This, however, seems to me to be a mere quibble, since "Si licet maleficos de medio tollere, ea spe et fine, ne hominibus amplius noceant per diabolum, ut ejus viva instrumenta; licet enim signa maleficii tollere, ne per diabolum illa amplius noceant, ut ejus fictitia instrumenta, non operantia quidem, sed eum ad operandum excitantia". The whole point is admirably argued by Delrio, *Disquisitionum Magicarum Libri Sex* (Lib. vi, cap. 2, sect. 1, quaestio 3),[178] who decides and indeed proves that one may most certainly seek out and destroy any instrument of witchcraft, any baleful charm, evil amulet, waxen puppet, witches' ladder, and the like, or any property upon which a spell has been cast, so that it has become or may become a conductor, dangerous and infect. I will go further and subscribe to Dominic Soto, who says that it is praiseworthy and meritorious to destroy these things, since thereby the charm is dissolved.[179] Girolamo Menghi, also, most highly approves of, and indeed urges, the destruction of this ensorcelled gear, whatever it may be: "non enim solum licet; sed etiam est meritorium destruere opera diaboli."[180] He justly terms all such questions as that of Sennert trifling and absurd.

Pietro Piperno, a physician of Benevento, who was also an excellent theologian, has written at length and very learnedly in his *De Magicis Affectibus, horum Dignotione, Prœnotione, Curatione, Medica, Stratagemmatica, Divina, plerique Curationibus Electis* (1634) of natural remedies and of superstitious charms and formulas in sickness. In chapter iv, book ii, he discusses: "Ut dæmon nocere desinat estne licitum, signum maleficiis destruere?" He lays down most emphatically: "Non enim solum licet, sed est meritorium destruere opera diaboli, nec in hoc est aliqua infidelitas, quia destruens non acquiescit operibus malignis, sed credit dæmonem posse, &

velle fatigare, dum tale durat signum, ac destructio tali signi finem imponit tali vexationi." He tells us, moreover, that the instruments of witchcraft must be burned, not destroyed in any other way, and "piis ceremoniis ea igne concremari melius est".[181] He holds that one may even request the witch to remove the spell and pay her money to calcinate and combust the periapts or ladders or figurines, since there will be no invocation of the dark powers whilst the intention is to put an end to and annul the effects of evil.

Piperno argues his case well and is undoubtedly in the right. Any object or instrument of sorcery should be burned, and it is important to get rid of and consign to the flames any articles which have been overlooked.

I have myself known so ordinary and commonplace a thing as a pair of curtains to which a spell was attached. A woman, afterwards known to have dealt in curious arts, who lived in a certain family, laid some charm upon a pair of blue richly brocaded curtains which usually hung in the drawing-room of the house. The curtains were of themselves costly and fine; they were handsome and much admired, so that the woman in question judged the family would never consent to replace them or pack them away out of use. When she left the service, which incidentally was in a disagreeable manner, the spell began to work. The family moved from one house to another, and in those years ill-luck always followed. The blue curtains naturally hung in each drawing-room window. At last, owing to various circumstances, suspicion was aroused. The curtains were taken down, and if not destroyed, have been discarded, and are carefully stored out of sight.

It is certain that evil may attach itself to possessions, to jewellery and gems, to objects of value and objects of comparatively no worth, to pictures, to miniatures and photographs, and, almost especially perhaps, to articles of furniture.

It may not be unfitting to give a striking example of this, as I have read and am very well assured is both recent and true.

A young couple, who live in a small but ancient coast town in Devonshire, after a courtship unmarred by any cloud, were married. The husband, who was about twenty-five years old, had worked with one firm for seven years, bearing a remarkably steady reputation. They spent a brief honeymoon in London, and then returned to their new home. One night, about a fortnight later, the young fellow came home completely intoxicated. His bride was aghast. The next day he was truly penitent, reproaching himself most bitterly. It was the first time that he had ever drunk to excess and he was usually content with just one glass of beer. About a month later they brought him home one night dead drunk. After this he was miserable and full of remorse. A few weeks later the same thing happened, he again got hopelessly drunk. His wife privately had recourse to a "wise woman" whom she consulted on the case. This sibyl came to the house and at once pointed to a certain piece of furniture, a large old-fashioned arm-chair, which had been given to the young couple as a wedding present, and in which the husband usually sat of an evening. "This is the trouble," said the wise woman. "It is all wrong. If you take my advice you will break it up and burn." The wife forthwith burned the chair, and after that all went well. Her husband never showed the slightest inclination to drink. The history of the chair was traced. It had once belonged to a butcher, who was a hardened drunkard, and who in a delirious fit had killed himself whilst sitting in it.[182] If such ill-luck befell in this case, what may not happen when the evil is directed and propelled of malice prepense and potent?

Sennert is of opinion that a man may justly resort to threats and blows in order to compel a witch to remove a spell or unlock a charm. It is indeed natural that one who has been harmed either in himself, those dear to him, or his goods, should adopt violent methods, and they are to my mind even praiseworthy, for he is thus showing his detestation of the witch, her master, and his abhorrence of the black art.

Pietro Piperno confirms this and writes: "Licet a malefico

petere, imo licet etiam ilium minis, & levibus verberibus cogere, ut maleficium tollat, quandocumque probabiliter credo ilium sine maleficio modo aliquo licito id facere posse sine quandocumque non sum moraliter certus quod utetur modo illicito."[183]

Benedict XIV, who was among the most learned of all the successors of S. Peter, debates whether a witch, terrified by threats and blows, commits a fresh sin by transferring to an ox (or any brute animal) the deadly spell she has cast upon the son of the man who trounced her. The conclusion is that the hag is guilty of a fresh sin inasmuch as she must have recourse to the demon to convey the spell from the sufferer and lay it elsewhere, whilst the father is in no wise to be held to blame since his only object is to save his child, and he is not bound to know by what methods the woman works.[184]

In January, 1928, a family of Hungarian peasants belonging to a village near Szegedin, were brought to trial at the assizes for causing the death of a witch. A spell was cast upon a farmer named Pittlik, who was seized by a mysterious sickness which in the course of months brought him wellnigh to the grave, and which the doctors were unable to cure. One night he saw a hag who caught him by the throat, and muttered some horrid blasphemy. His relatives resolved to watch for the witch, and accordingly night after night they lay in wait. About a week passed, when there came one midnight a soft tapping and an aged woman crept into the room. The watchers flung themselves on her with sticks and axes, but unfortunately deprived her of life. Nevertheless, from that moment Pittlik was completely cured. The court justly acquitted the accused since the case pointed to the existence of a witch, and they had acted under irresistible compulsion. At a second trial for homicide the family were sentenced to short terms of imprisonment, which were reduced by the supreme court. I understand a third trial was ordered.[185]

Not long ago a Devonshire farmer attacked a woman, reputed as a witch, scratched her with a pin until she bled, and threatened to shoot her, inasmuch as she had ill-wished him and cast a spell on his pig.[186]

The concluding chapters of his work Sennert devotes to the natural remedies which must be tried in cases of sickness through ensorcelling, and the drugs and treatment, which fortunately enough in very many instances are found to be effectual. But it is highly advisable also that, if there be manifest signs of some supernormal malady, strange, irregular, and unusual symptoms, the aid of the Church be required, yet not upon any light cause or occasion. In his final chapter, *De divina curatione*, the doctor writes with a good deal of unction of exorcism.[187]

I have, of course, in this survey only taken up a few points of interest and importance from the *De Morbis Occultis*, and I do not pretend to give a digest or even a conspectus of the whole tract, which in fine I do not consider save in so far as it concerns us here.

Pietro Piperno touches very lightly upon lycanthropy, and seems inclined to suppose that it is not due to demoniacal possession. He has been misled here by Weyer, for he writes: "De lycantropia, seu lupina insania Arabibus Chatrab. unde Avicen. lib. 3. F. 1. T. 4.15. appellavit quamdam maniam daemoniacam; Leoninam vel avinam, vel caninam, &c. monstrantem signa fere obsessi Ovid 1. metamorph. sic depingebat . . . qua melancolie refert Forestus lib. 10. obs. 19. auctoritate Vuierij, multi doctissimi viri Medici decepti sunt ad affirmandum morbum esse daemoniacum."[188]

Having established then at least a probable opinion that lycanthropy, *daemonium lupinum*, is for the most part, if indeed not invariably, of the nature of possession, before we proceed to discuss the actual transformation of men into wolves, the methods and possibility of such metamorphosis, it will not be impertinent briefly to consider this disease, which the Greeks termed λυκανθρωπία, which has by more than one writer erroneously been supposed the tradition of the werewolf, and to review the opinions of certain great medical writers from the beginning.

Marcellus Sidetes, a native of Side in Pamphylia, who was born towards the end of the first century, and lived in the reigns of Hadrian and Antoninus Pius, A.D. 117–161,[189] is famous as the author of a long medical poem in Greek hexameter verse, which was so highly esteemed that, as Suidas tells us, the emperors commanded that all public libraries in Rome must be furnished with a copy.[190] Unfortunately only two fragments of this work remain, Περὶ Λυκανθρώπου, De Lycanthropia, and Ἰατρικὰ περὶ Ἰχθύων, De Bemediis ex Piscibus. The De Lycanthropia is preserved, but in a prose version only, by the Greek doctor Aëtius, who compiled an encyclopædic work on medicine from the writings of many authors now no longer extant, for which reason rather than for any original matter the Βιβλία Ἰατρικὰ Ἑκκαίδεκα are valued. Maximilian Schneider writes: "Ex tanta Marcelli Sidetae librorum copia nihil ad nostra tempora servatum est nisi duo vel tria fragmenta . . . Quantum fragmentum Marcelli Περὶ λυκανθρωπίας servatum est in Aetii Iatr. vi, 11 (editum ab J. G. Schneidero, I.E. p. 109 seq. et Kuehnio, I.c. i, p. 7), sed ita ut numeri resoluti sint in orationem pedestrem."[191] Johann Gottlieb Schneider (p. 109) gives: "Marcelli Sidetae Fragmentum Περὶ Λυκανθρώπου quod exstat apud Aëtium S. 6, p. 104 b. περὶ λυκανθρώπου ἤτοι κυνανθρώπου, et apud Paulum Æginet. 3, p. 30 b. qui tacito nomine autoris haec repetiit, περὶ λυκάονος ἢ λυκανθρώπου"[192] Since Schneider thus refers to Paulus Ægineta,[193] who has but conveyed the earlier work of Marcellus Sidetes, we may turn to the later writer, and it will not be amiss to quote the excellent translation by Francis Adams,[194] who Englished *The Seven Books of Paulus Ægineta* with an ample commentary for the Sydenham Society, three volumes, London, 1844.

The passage in question[195] is the sixteenth section of book iii: "On Lycaon, or Lycanthropia. Those labouring under lycanthropia go out during the night imitating wolves in all things and lingering about sepulchres until morning. You may recognize such persons by these marks: they are pale, their vision feeble, their eyes dry, tongue very dry, and the flow of the saliva stopped; but they are thirsty, and their legs have incurable ulcerations from frequent falls. Such are the marks of the disease. You must know that lycanthropia is a species of melancholy which you may cure at the time of the attack, by opening a vein and abstracting blood to fainting, and giving the patient a diet of wholesome food. Let him use baths of sweet water, and then milk-whey for three days, and purging with the hiera from colocynth twice or thrice. After the purgings use the theriac of vipers, and administer those things mentioned for the cure of melancholy. [Dodder of thyme, *epithymus*; aloes; wormwood after purging; acrid vinegar as a beverage; squills, poley, slender birthwort; phlebotomy and cataplasms. In chronic cases evacuation, by vomiting with hellebore.] When the disease is already formed, use soporific embrocations, and rub the nostrils with opium when going to rest."

Adams comments[196]: "See Aëtius (vi, 11); Oribasius (Synops. viii, 10); Actuarius (Mett. Med. i, 16); Anonymus (de Lycanth. ap. Phys. et Med. Min.); Psellus (Carm. de Re Med. ibid.); Avicenna (iii, 1, 5, 22); Haly Abbas (Theor. ix, 7, Pract. v, 24); Alsaharavius (Pract. 1, 2, 28); Rhases (Divis. 10, Cont. 1). All the other authorities give much the same account of this species of melancholy as Paulus . . . Avicenna recommends the application of the actual cautery to the sinciput when the other remedies fail. Haly Abbas describes the disease by the name of *melancholia canina*. He says the patient delights to wander among tombs, imitating the cries of dogs; that his colour is pale; his eyes misty (tenebricosi), dry, and hollow; his mouth parched; and that he has marks on his limbs of injuries which he has sustained from falls. He recommends the same treatment as our author: indeed he evidently merely translates this section of Paulus. Alsaharavius seems also to allude to this disease by the name of *melancholia canina*. Rhases' account of it is quite similar to our author's."

Of Aëtius we have just spoken. Oribasius was probably born about A.D. 325. Suidas and Philostorgius call him a native of Sardes in Lydia, but Eunapius, who was his friend, writes that he was born at Pegamus in Mysia, the native place of Galen. However that may be, Oribasius early acquired a great professional reputation, and was a particular favourite with Julian the Apostate, although under the succeeding emperors he was justly exiled owing to his enmity against the Christians. He was living at least as late as A.D. 395, when Eunapius inserted his life in the *Vitae Philosphorum et Sophistarum*. Of Oribasius three extant works are considered genuine. Reference is here made to the Σύνοψις in nine books. It has never been published in the original Greek, but a Latin version by Joannes Baptista Rasarius was printed at Venice, 8vo, 1554.

Joannes Actuarius lived at Constantinople towards the end of the thirteenth century. His *De Methedo Medendi*, in six books, has only been printed in a Latin translation by Cornelius H. Mathisius, which first appeared at Venice, 4to, 1554. His works are included in the *Medicae Artis Principes* of H. Stephens, Paris, folio, 1567.[197]

The *De Lycanthropia*, Περι λυκανθρωπίας, is merely a brief abstract or synopsis of Paulus Ægineta. It will be found in Julius Ludwig Ideler's *Physici et Medici Graeci Minores*, Berlin, 1842, vol. ii.[198] In the same collection is included the *Carmen de Re Medica* of Psellus the Sophist.[199] The lines in question, 837–841, run:—

Μελάγχολόν τι πρᾶγμα λυκανθρωπία.
Ἔστι γὰρ αὐτόχρημα μισανθρωπία.
Καὶ γνωριεῖς ἄνθρωπον εἰσπεπτωκότα,
Ὁρῶν περιτρί ντα νυκτὸς τοὺς τάΟους,
Ὠχρόν, κατηΟ , ζηρόν, ἠμελημένον.[200]

Of Avicenna, "un phénomène intellectuel" (980–1036); Haly Abbas (Ali-ben-el-Abbas) who died 994–5; Alsaharavius (Albucasis, Aboul Cassem Khalef ben Abbas Essahraouy), whose great work is conveniently known as the *Tesrif* (*Practice*); and Razès (Abou Beer Mohammed ben Zakarya), who died at a great age in 923; full accounts may be found in Dr. Lucien Leclerc's

Histoire de la Médecine Arabe.[201]

Of older physicians one may also consult Marcellus Donatus, *De Medica Historia Mirabili*,[202] Liber vi, c. 1, and a writer of later date, Petrus Salius, *De Affectibus Particularibus*, "De Febre Pestilenti Tractatus," c. xix, *De Rabie*.[203]

Robert Burton, speaking of lycanthropia, says: "Some make a doubt whether there be any such disease," which indeed seems a strange thing in the face of history, for not only do very many of the Saints and Fathers and other gravest authors record such terrible happenings, but we also have the testimony of the Sacred Scripture itself. "*This malady*, saith *Avicenna*, troubleth men most in February, and is now-a-days frequent in Bohemia and Hungary, according to Heurnius. Schernitzius will have it common in Livonia."[204]

To Jan van Hewin (Heurne, Heurnius), the celebrated Dutch physician who was born at Utrecht 25th January, 1543, and died at Leyden 11th August, 1601, reference has already been made. He wrote many medical treatises which were accepted as of great authority. The *De Morbis qui in singulis partibus humani capitis incidere consueverunt* was first printed at Leyden 1594, 4to. The rubric of chapter xiii runs: "*De* Mania, *id est, Insania, aut Furore vel Ecstasi Melancholica*," and the last paragraph deals with lycanthropy. "Lycanthropia (λνκάων) qualis sit affectio primum diximus. dicitur Arabibus chatrab, sumpto nomine a bestiola quae sine serie certa super aquas hue & illuc fertur: ita hi etiam stare loco nesciunt. Refert D. Schenckius (*Historia mira*) ex Io. Fincelio, libro 2. Mirac, hanc historiam. Patavii lupus sibi videbatur agricola anno 1541. Multosque in agris insiliit, trucidavitque. Tandem non sine difficultate captus, confidenter se asseveravit verum esse lupum, discrimen solum existere in pelle cum pilis inuersa. Quapropter gladiis feriunt eius tibias & brachia, amputantque, veritatem rei exploraturi. Cognito vero hominis errore, eum chirurgis tradunt curandum, sed post dies non multos exspiravit." Van Hewin then diagnoses the symptoms of lycanthropy, and prescribes the remedies, medicated baths, a light diet with milk, senna, and other drugs. If necessary, the cautery.

The well-known Johann Weyer, in his *De iis, qui Lamiarum Maleficio affecti putantur,* devotes chapter xxiii to lycanthropy: "De λνκανθρωπία morbo, quo se in lupos converti credunt homines"[205] He is more cautious here than in many passages of this work, and indeed his chapter is largely a paraphrase of the older authorities, especially Paulus Ægineta. Weyer describes the symptoms very exactly, and recommends much the same course of treatment, although he is perhaps a little more detailed in the account of the various remedies. He also quotes William of Brabant, and the famous history given by Job Fincel. We shall have occasion to return to Weyer when dealing with other aspects of lycanthropy.

Weyer is quoted, and indeed largely drawn upon, by Johann Georg Schenck, a celebrated physician of Fribourg, where he was born towards the end of the sixteenth century. The son of Johann Schenck of Graffenberg, he rather grandiloquently describes himself as "a Grafenberg Philiater, Hagenoensium Alsatiae Poliater, Comitisque ab Hanaw Physicus Medicus". In his *Observationum Medicarum, Rararum, Novarum, Admirabilium, et Monstrosarum Tomus,* Frankfort, 1600, liber i, Observatio cclx, he treats *De Lycanthropia.* "Lycanthropia seu lupinae insaniae exempla horribilia." Actually Schenck only repeats and refers to the former authorities. He cites Altomari, Aëtius, Paulus Ægineta, Job Fincel, and others, including (as we have noted) Weyer. Schenck notes: "Id nostro hoc seculo cuidam Hispano nobili oblatum fuisse edendum traditur, qui per deserta ac montes vagabatur; se in ursum esse conversum phantasia vitiata ratus."

Joannes Arculanus of Verona in his *Practica* (Venice, Giunta, 1557, folio) in his *In Nonum Librum Almansoris Expositio,* caput xvi, *De melancholia,*[206] treats at length of that species of melancholia which "Avicenna terms cutubutt". "Mania vero est duplex una lupina, aliter dicta daemonium lupinum, videntur enim non homines sed daemones et lupi, qui patiuntur hanc maniam." This great physician has indeed here put his finger upon the spot, and discerns the whole truth of the matter in a few words, since the patients suffering from this diabolical werewolfery "seem in very truth to be men no longer but incarnate devils and ravening wolves". He also speaks of the second kind of mania, "mania canina ad canum similitudinem." "Sed causa maniae lupinae est melancholia genita per adustionem cholerae, aut melancholiae, & est deterior, quia difficilioris curationis, cum humor genitus per adustionem melancholiae fit magis crassus, ineptior digestioni & resolutioni & evacuationi. Et signa ejus sunt agitatio, saltus, inquisitio, lupinositas, id est mores luporum, & aspectus cui non assimilatur aspectus hominis, imo est sicut luporum. Differt etiam ab una specie karabiti quae est cum daemonio, quoniam cum hac mania non est febris sed karabitus est cum se."

A little later he continues: "Cutubut . . . nomen sumpsit a quadam specie araneæ quae movetur super aqua diversis motibus sine ordine. [The water-spider, *tipula*.] . . . Cutubut autem est species melancholiae plurimum eveniens in februario, non exspectans usque ad ver, propter subtilitatem humoris melancholici plurimum . . . haec enim diligit fugere ab hominibus vivis et approprinquare mortuis et sepulchris cum malitia furoris repente advenientis ei. Et est ejus processio nocturna, & occultatio diurna. Et totum istud facit diligendo solitutidem et elongationem ab hominibus. Et cum hoc non quiescit in uno loco plus una hora, imo non cessat discurrere et ambulare incessione diversa ignorans quo vadit cavendo sibi ab hominibus. . . . Et citrinus est color faciei. Et lingua sicut sitientis. Et super crura ipsius sunt ulcera quae non consolidantur. . . . Et oculi ejus sunt sicci, debiles, submersi, non lachrymantes propter siccitatem cerebri et oculorum."

Arculanus discusses the remedies for lycanthropy, *De cura cuthubutt*,[207] at considerable length. In addition to the usual remedies and courses for melancholia he insists upon the necessity for sleep and repose, and further advises bloodletting, "copiosior phlebotomia . . . multa extractio sanguinis." He concludes: "Quantum [remedium] est ut verberetur cum hic sit multum inobediens."

It may be remarked that Bernard Gordonius recommends the same somewhat drastic treatment; "colaphizetur et flagilletur" are his words.[208]

Richard Argentine, in his *De Praestigiis et Incantationibus Daemonum*,[209] emphasizes the use of natural remedies in cases of possession, that the black bile of the sufferer may be purged with hellebore: "Nam lunatici ut ait Coelius Rhodiginus eorum intelligantur nomine qui dicuntur ἐνεργούμενοι, hoc est obsessi, velut in eos agat μήνυ, hoc est luna, in quibus per atram bilem imaginationi mancipatus animus, facile immundorum spirituum fit conceptaculum, et daemoniacam virtutem nanciscitur, quam Eusebius Paredrum dici affirmat, alii assesorem. Daemoniacos praeterea veteres vocabant a nimia capitis humectatione, Cerebrique humorum exuberantia hygrocephalos, inde a nostris quoque maioribus lymphationis nomen ductum est, ut vicio hoc affecti vocentur Lymphatici etiam pro Nymphatici, quod genus morbi lycaones et lycanthropos facit, cynanthropos et melancholicos feros et immanes. Et exorcistae inquit idem qui spiritus per Orationes sanctorum et aspersione aquae benedictae fugare profitentur, primo euacuant sic laborantes ab atra bile."

Girolamo Mercuriale, in his *Medicina Practica*, lib. i, cap. xii, *De Lykanthropia*, treating of the complaint, says: "Assuredly this is a most terrible disease, and yet not necessarily fatal, not even if it last for months. Indeed I have read that after several years it was completely cured. The treatment is the same as that when dealing with lunacy." The Arab physicians recommend copious blood-letting, moreover they advise castigation and many stripes.

Luigi Celio Ricchieri in his *Lectionum Antiquarum Libri Triginta*,[210] lib. xxvii, c. 12, has but a passing notice of lycanthropy: "Est item melancholica affectio, dicta Graecis λυκανθρωπια, et qui sic officiuntur, Lycanthropi, quoniam lupos imitari prorsum videantur. Exsiliunt quippe noctu, adque diem usque inter sepulchra diversantur. Eorum praepallet facies, καὶ ὄρω σιν ἀδρανὲς, oculis arescentibus, praecipue vero lingua. Sunt praeterea διψώδεις, hoc est sitibundi: tibiis ex impactione crebra ἀνιάτως, id est citra medelam ulcerosis. Hosce etiam Lycaonas dici, observavimus."

Pierre van Foreest, the eminent Dutch physician, who was born at Alkmaer in 1552 and died there 1597, in his *Observation num . . . Medicinae Theoricae et Practicae Libri XXVIII*,[211] closely follows Joannes Arculanus. Observatio xxv of the tenth book *De Cerebri Morbis* has for rubric *De lycanthropia seu lupina insania*. It is of especial interest as he gives a case which came under his own notice at Alkmaer. A peasant was noticed in the spring-time to be roving about the streets of the town in a peculiar and indecisive manner. His looks were fierce and frantic. After prowling up and down in the cemetery he entered a church, where van Foreest carefully watched his antics (*ut ipsi spectavimus*). He leaped to and fro over the benches, danced wildly, rushed to and fro in the nave and aisles, and could not remain still for a moment. In one hand he held a great club, which he used to keep off any dog he might see in his path, although he neither approached nor attacked individuals. It was remarked that his bare legs, unwashen and filthy, were scarred with the bites of dogs and old ulcerated sores. His body was gaunt, his limbs squalid and foul with neglect, his face ghastly pale, the eyes deep-sunken, dry, and blazing. From these symptoms van Foreest judged that the man was a lycanthrope, but so far as could be discovered he was under no doctor's care. He avoided, indeed, as far as possible the gaze of men, and fled away secretly by himself.

In his *Scholia* van Foreest discusses the disease and its remedies at length, and gives a careful and interesting account of this malady, although perhaps he does not add anything very vital to the observations of his predecessors. He remarks, indeed, that sufferers often imagine themselves to have assumed other animal forms besides that of a wolf. "Plerosque etiam atra bile vitiatos se leones esse, vel daemones, vel aves imaginari, annotavit Avicenna."[212]

Donato Antonio Altomari, the celebrated Neapolitan physician and philosopher, who was born in the first quarter of the sixteenth century, has a chapter, *Περὶ λυκανθρωπίας*, *De lupina insania*, in his treatise *De Medendis Humani Corporis Malis*,[213] which he wrote in 1560 and dedicated to Pope Paul IV. Altomari draws chiefly from Aëtius and Paulus Ægineta, to whom he refers the student. He agrees that the disease is at its worst in February and mentions two patients whom he has treated successfully. One of these he encountered on a certain day in the streets. The lycanthropist, who was raving, had been violating a graveyard and was clutching members he had torn from a corpse. "Ipsi quidem ferebat humeris crus integrum, ac tibiam defuncti cuiusdam." Altomari notes: "Qui namque hoc affectu detinentur in Februario mense noctu domo egressi lupos in curatis imitantur, & donee dies illucescat, circa defunctorum monumenta vagantur, eaque maxime aperiunt." He emphasizes as notable symptoms an excessive parching thirst, and a complete loss of memory of the attacks after recovery.

Bartolomeo Castelli, a famous physician of Messina, in his well-known *Lexicon medicum*, writes of lycanthropes as follows: "Aegri noctu domo egressi, urbem circumeunt, quadrupedum more incidentes, lupos imitantur ululantes, donee dies illucescat, defunctorum monumenta quaeritant, adaperiunt, cadauerum frusta arripientes, secumque collo gestantes, fugiuntque die uiuos homines, nocte insequentes mortuos. Sunt autem eorum notae: facies pallida, oculi sicci et caui, uisus hebes, lingua siccissima, saliua in ore nulla, sitis immodica, tibiae perpetuo exulceratae propter frequentes casus. Nonnulli etiam ut canes mordent, ex quo arbitror, morbum ipsum *κυνανδρωπίαν* uocatum fuisse ueteribus."[214]

Petrus Salius mentions that those who eat the roast flesh of a wolf that happens to be mad will be attacked by the disease.[215] He describes certain of the symptoms of the lycanthrope: "Spuma ad os eis apparet, dentibus alios petunt, ut canes latrant, vel ut lupi ululant, dentibus strident, sudant, et convelluntur."[216] We have here the very symptoms of demoniacal possession as in Holy Writ. When Our Lord came down from the Mount of Transfiguration the man from the crowd thus described the effects of possession in his son: "Lo, a spirit seizeth him, and he suddenly crieth out, and he throweth him down and teareth him, so that he foameth; and bruising him, he hardly departeth from him." These exact details are, it will be remembered, recorded by S. Luke the physician.

Menghi in his *Complementum Artis Exorcisticae* lists among the "Signa Daemoniaci": "14. Stridunt dentibus, spumant, ac signa alia ostendunt tanquam Canes rabidi."[217]

Salius lays especial stress upon the detail that lycanthropes avoid water: "aquam perhorrescunt." It were too curious to inquire how far this unnatural dread of clear water is psychologically connected with the water ordeal to which those suspected of sorcery were so often submitted. The history of the "*judicium aquae frigidae*" is long and interesting, but here we need only touch upon it very briefly. Running water in particular is known to dissolve spells and evil charms; true and natural water is the matter of the "first sacrament", "the door of the spiritual life".[218] Thus the element has of itself a certain quality of holiness. "Living water," the Hebrews of old called it.

Water was appointed as a test in cases of sorcery as early as the laws of Hammurabi, King of Babylon, in the third millennium B.C.,[219] and in England the water ordeal is ancient, a full description of this test being given in the Laws of Aethelstan, 924–940.[220] Other codes mention it, and the test was essayed for theft, adultery, and homicide as well as witchcraft. The Fourth Lateran Council, however, in 1215, under Innocent III, by its nineteenth canon forbade priests to pronounce any benedictions at the ordeals of hot or cold water and of the hot iron. There had been grave abuses, whilst in any case the experiment was not wholly trustworthy.

Nevertheless the ordeal itself persisted, so deep-rooted in the rustic mind was a belief in the completest efficacy of "swimming a witch". Particularly in England and in Germany did the populace favour the practice. In the sixteenth century King James judged that "their fleeting on the water" was appointed by God "for a super-naturall signe of the monstruous impietie of the Witches, that the water shal refuse to receiue them in her bosom, that haue shaken off them the sacred Water of Baptisme, and wilfullie refused the benefite thereof".[221]

This, however, was flatly denied by William Perkins (1558–1602) in his *A Discourse of the Damned Art of Witchcraft*, published posthumously in 1608 by Thomas Pickering, minister of Finchingfield in Essex, who writes: "And yet to iustifie the casting of a Witch into the water, it is alledged, that hauing made a couenant with the deuill, shee hath renounced her Baptisme, and hereupon there growes an Antipathie betweene her, and water. *Ans.* This allegation serues to no purpose: for all water is not the water of Baptisme, but that onely which is vsed in the very act of Baptisme, and not before nor after. The element out of the vse of the Sacrament, is no Sacrament, but returnes again to his common vse."[222]

Owing to the activities of the errant and unlicensed witch-finders, swimming even in England presently fell into general disrepute during the seventeenth century. Even Matthew Hopkins was obliged to acknowledge that in his high noon the ordeal is by able divines "condemned for no way, and therefore of late hath, and for ever shall be left".[223] None the less the mobile swum witches in England pretty frequently throughout the eighteenth century, and not unseldom indeed during the nineteenth. A particularly notorious case occurred in 1863, at Castle Headingham in Essex,[224] and the *Daily Telegraph*, 23rd June, 1880,[225] reports that at Dunmow Petty Sessions, Charles and Peter Brewster, father and son, were bound over to keep the peace for six months on a charge of molesting Susan Sharpe, the wife of an army pensioner, living at High Easter. The two

Brewsters wanted to put her to the test by throwing her in a pond to see if she would sink or swim. The young defendant declared that he and his wife were bewitched. The furniture in their house was disturbed and moved uneasily; their domestic animals died in extraordinary ways; shadows appeared in their bedroom, some of which bore an uncanny resemblance to Mrs. Sharpe. They had consulted several "cunning men and women" in the neighbourhood, apparently with no result, save that everything pointed to Mother Susan as the cause of their troubles. I have no doubt at all that here was a clear case of witchcraft, and that Mrs. Sharpe was a sorceress of the tribe of Ursley Kempe, Julian Cox, and Rose Cullender.

We can hardly be surprised that hag-ridden rustics should resort to the old—if dishonoured—traditional test for discovering their tormentor's guilt. That theologians and physicians looked askance at such rough and ready methods the vulgar little recked.

Jan van Hewin categorically denied that this fleeting on the water was any proof of witchcraft. "Nullum esse aquae innatationem Lamiarum indicium," are his words, and he proceeds to give his reasons for such a judgment, although it must be confessed these are not perhaps entirely convincing.[226] What is far more important with reference to this ordeal is the pronouncement of Benedict XIV when he wrote: "In Westphaliae regionibus ea superest corruptela, ut in sagas, atque veneficos inquireretur, eos dejiciendo in aquam frigidam, ita manibus pedibusque ligatis, ut, cum natare non valerent, ei submergerentur, innocentes censerentur, si vero supernaterent, pro reis haberentur. At id ipsum quoque nunc de medio sublatum, et a Judicibus hujusmodi experimenta proscripta fuerunt."[227] No contrary opinion must be maintained in the face of this prelection, but it may be noted that the Pope speaks of swimming a witch only as "corruptela" and as an experiment. We are free, perhaps, to consider it a test, although by no means a satisfactory test, a mere experiment, and historically it is an essay which has led to scenes of mob violence that are greatly to be deplored, on which account, chiefly, the Holy Father suppresses and forbids any such trial.

A WEREWOLF ATTACKS A MAN

King James points out that save "at euery light occasion . . . dissemblingly" the witch cannot shed tears.[228] Here we are on safer ground. For from the *Malleus Maleficarum*, part iii, question 15, we learn that a witch is unable to weep, and why.[229] Grillandus[230] and Bodin[231] agree with Sprenger in this particular, but Bishop Binsfeld,[232] Godelmann,[233] and Delrio[234] more than doubt. The point is a nice one, but whatever authority we follow it is significant that Joannes Arculanus particularly draws attention to the fact that the eyes of the lycanthrope are hot and dry, and that he cannot shed a tear.[235]

Precisely the same symptom is emphasized by Daniel Sennert, who in his *Practica Medicina*, lib. i, pars. ii, c. xiv, distinguishes "Melancholia errabunda, Arabibus Kutubutt dicta" from lycanthropia.[236]

He notes that "Melancholia errabunda medicis dicta, ea melancholiae species est, quae plerumque Februario mense aegros infestare solit; nomenque hoc accipit, quod qui ea laborant, ne horam in uno loco quiescere possunt, sed hinc inde continuò vagantur nescientes tamen quò vadunt", which are indeed the very features Arculanus, Van Foreest, and others regard as indicative of lycanthropy. According to Sennert the appearance of the sufferer is that of the lycanthropist. "Color corporis est citrinus, lingua sicca, ut valde sitientis, oculi sicci, concavi, nunquam lacrymantes." Moreover, "solitulidem amant, noctu magis vagantur, latebras circa mortuorum sepulchra et alia loca solitaria, quaerunt. Homines obvios fugiunt." He mentions that the legs are ulcerated, but assigns a different reason for this: "cum ob continuum motum melancholia ad crura descendat."

Lycanthropia, Sennert defines as a kind of madness, "quando aegri unius bestiae mores in specie referunt, quod etiam plerumque a veneno et morsu talium bestiarum rabibadarum communicatur et inducitur, qualis est Lycanthropia, rabies canina, lupina ac felina."[237]

Dr. L.-F. Calmeil, in his well-known work *De La Folie*, certainly classes lycanthropy among the "folies démoniaques", which is something. He writes: "La zoanthropie doit aussi prendre rang parmi les espèces de folies démoniaques . . . les malades qui en ont été affectés en plus grand nombre prétendaient avoir fait des pactes avec Lucifer, et avoir obtenu de lui le pouvoir de se transformer en hiboux, en chats on en loups, pour se gorger plus facilement de sang et de chair. Plusieurs de ces individus s'imaginaient être couverts de poils, avoir eu pour armes des griffes et des dents redoutables, avoir déchiré, dans leurs courses nocturnes, des hommes ou des animaux, avoir sucé le sang des nourrissons au berceau, avoir commis meurtres sur meurtres. Quelques lycanthropes ont été surpris en pleine campagne marchant sur leurs mains et sur leurs genoux, imitant la voix des loups, tout souillés de boue, de sueur, haletans, emportant des débris de cadavres. On peut donc présumer que quelques uns d'entre eux ait pu immoler à leur appétit des êtres vivans; mais presque tous s'accusaient de crimes qui n'avaient jamais été en réalité commis, commes ils se vantaient aussi d'avoir couvert des louves, d'avoir course certaines nuits sous la forme d'un lièvre.

"Les lycanthropes étaient quelquefois dans un état assez semblable à l'état extatique lorsque leur cerveau enfantait les hallucinations et les autres conceptions que nous venons de relater ... La zoanthropie a régné successivement dans beaucoup de contrées; elle s'y est souvent manifestée sur un certain nombre de malades à la fois; les pays déserts et à demi-sauvages ont été surtout le théâtre de atte espèce de folie."[238]

We may now pass to a very striking case of lycanthropy which has been recorded of more recent years, and the details of which are given by Dr. Daniel Hack Tuke in his *Dictionary of Psychological Medicine*.[239] The sufferer in question came under the care of Dr. Morel, who described the case in *Études Cliniques*,[240] 1852. This unfortunate individual was entirely convinced that he had assumed the form of a wolf. "See this mouth," he would exclaim, separating his lips with his fingers, "it is the mouth of a wolf; these are the teeth of a wolf. I have cloven feet; see the long hairs which cover my body; let me run into the woods, and you shall shoot me!" During his quieter intervals he was sometimes allowed to see children whom he tenderly embraced, and of whom he was very fond. However, after they had gone he cried, "The unfortunates, they have hugged a wolf!"

He was a victim to the morbid wolfish hunger which is technically known as lycorexia or lycorrhexis. "Give me raw meat," he was wont to yell, "I am a wolf, a wolf!" When he was supplied with this, he would greedily devour some part, and reject the rest saying that it was not putrid enough.

This lycanthrope endured the most fearful mental agony, accusing himself of and tortured by the guilt of heinous offences which he certainly had not committed. He died at the asylum of Maréville in a state of marasmus, seemingly in the uttermost spiritual dereliction. But this, we may hope, was the climax of his trial, for there appears little doubt from reading the details of the case that here we have a plain case of diabolical possession. It is unfortunate, indeed, that a skilled exorcist was not summoned to deal with the patient.

There can be few histories more melancholy, more terribly sad. But throughout all this darkness we may find comfort in the words of that great pope, Benedict XIV: "Daemones dum homines obsident, in corpora potissimum potestatem habere et exercere, in animas vero non ita multum posse; et finitam et certam esse eorum potestatem in ipsa corpora obsessorum quia quemadmodum non nisi obtenta a Deo facultate, corpora ingrediuntur, ita eorum corporibus plus damni afferre non possunt quam a Deo Optimo Maximo illis permittatur et praefiniatur."[241]

FOOTNOTESI

1 Vol. ii (1931), p. 475.

2 The Master of Game, c. 1400. Bodleian; Digby MS. 182; vi.

3 Jamieson, Etymological Dictionary of the Scottish Language, 1808, vol. ii, s.v. Warwolf, Werwouf.

4 The famous Catholic antiquary, c. 1560–1625.

5 Abraham Orteil or Œrtel, the Flemish scholar and geographer, born 1527, died at Antwerp 1598. "The Ptolemy of the sixteenth century." Verstigan refers to the Aurei seculi imago sive Germanorum veterun mores.

6 Delrio mentions this case of werewolfism in his Disquisitionum Magicarum Libri Sex, ii, quaestio xviii (1599). In the edition of 1603 "nunc secundis curis auctior longe", Moguntiae, folio, the reference will be found on pp. 165–6. There is an allusion to Peter Stump in Samuel Rowlands, The Knave of Harts. Haile Fellow well met, 4to, 1612 (p. 47), the Epigram preceding the Epilogue. Another reference to "the late accidents in the Netherlands of Stub Peter and others, which Witches that

people do call weary wolves" occurs in the Fairfax Discourse of Witchcraft or Discourse of Daemonology (1621), ed. R. M. Milnes, Philobiblon Society, London, 1858-9, vol. v, No. 3, pp. 176-180.

7 Bedburg on the river Erft near Cologne is at the present day a town of 2,925 inhabitants.

8 Ed. 1927, pp. 181-4.

9 Ibid., p. 182, n. 2.

10 George Turberville, The Noble Art of Venerie or Hunting. Printed with the Booke of Faulconrie, or Hawking, 4to, 1575 and 4to, 1611. Art of Venerie, lxxv, 206: "Some Wolues . . . kill children and men sometimis: and then they neuer feede nor pray vpon any thing afterwards . . . Such Wolues are called War-wolues, bicause a man had neede to beware of them." It has not been recognized that Turberville is merely quoting from the older Booke of Huntynge (c. 1400).

11 Ancient Laws and Institutes of England, ed. B. Thorpe, 1840, pp. 160-1. The old Latin version, Quadripartitus, of xxvi (p. 535), runs: "Sane sunt episcopi et sacerdotes qui gregem Domini sapienti doctrina debent custodire et defendere, ne diabolica vesania ilium vulneret vel occidat." Felix Liebermann, Die Gesetze der Angelsachsen, vol. i, Halle, 1903, p. 307, Consiliatio Cnuti, supplies another Latin version which thus turns this passage: "hii sunt episcopi et presbiteri, qui divinam custodiam patrocinari tutarique debent supientibus doctrinis, ne forte ille dementer avidus virlupus supra modum a divina custodia dirripiat et mortificet." Cnut, King of Denmark, became King of all England on the death of Edmund Ironsides 1017, and ruled until his decease in 1035.

12 Asser's Life of King Alfred, ed. W. H. Stevenson, Oxford, 1904, c. 77, pp. 62-3, and notes on that passage, pp. 304-5.

13 This nineteenth book Corrector was frequently circulated as a separate treatise, a manual for confessors. Von Scherer, Kirchenrecht, i, 238.

14 Burchard, Decretorum libri XX, Coloniae, 1548, "opus nunc

primum excussum," p. 198, verso, De incredulis. Migne, Pair. Lat., clx, p. 971. See also H. J. Schmitz, Die Bussbücher und die Bussdisciplin der Kirche, Mainz, 1883, pp. 714, 718.

15 See Montague Summers, The History of Witchcraft, 1926, pp. 16–18, 20–8, and passim.

16 Historiarum Libri Quinque, Lib. iv, c. 11. "De haeresi in Italia inventa," apud Migne, Pair. Lat., cxlii, p. 672.

17 Sermo xv. Migne, Patr. Lat., lxxxix, p. 870.

18 Otia Imperialia . . . ed. Felix Liebrecht, Hanover, 1856. xv. De oculis apertis post peccatum, p. 4.

19 Sixth Earl of Hereford, nephew to Edward II and first cousin to Edward III. Humphrey de Bohun succeeded his brother John as Earl on 20th January, 1336, and died unmarried 15th October, 1361.

20 William of Palerne, ed. W. W. Skeat, Early English Text Society, 1867, p. 9. A plural "werwolfs" occurs in 1. 2540 (p. 85).

21 Ed. Skeat, E.E.T.S., 1867, p. 17, 11. 458–60.

22 Morte Darthur, ed. H. Oskar Sommer, 1889, vol. i, p. 793. Malory's work was first printed by Caxton, folio, 1485.

23 The earliest known printed text (quoted here) of the Fabillis is 4to, 1570. There are various MSS., Harleian, Makculloch, Bannatyne, Asloan-Chalmers. See Poems of Robert Henryson, Scottish Text Society, vol. ii, 1906, ed. G. Gregory Smith, who curiously enough does not furnish a note on this passage (vol. ii, p. 66, l. 881), which most certainly requires an ample excursus.

24 Walter Kennedy (1460?–1508?). "Flyting" is a literary war of words, which might be more or less serious. Adversaries assuredly did not spare the sharpest invective and coarse abuse.

25 Poems of William Dunbar, S.T.S., part i, 1883–4, ed. Dr. John Small, p. 19, 11. 249–53: "Syphaerit" means reduced to a cypher, i.e. nothing, and thus having no place among the Saints of Heaven.

26 Sir Patrick Hume of Polwarth, a favourite of King James VI. Hume died 15th June, 1609. Alexander Montgomerie, c.

1545–c. 1610.

27 This is the reading of the Tullibardine MS.; Harleian MS. has:
Ane warlocke, ane warwoolffe, Ane volbet but hair,
Ane devill, and a dragon, ane deid dromadarrie . . .
See Poems of Alexander Montgomerie, S.T.S., ed. George
Stevenson, 1910, pp. 174–5, 11. 600–1.

28 This is the reading of the Harleian MS., the Tullibardine MS.
has: "With wolfis and wilcattes." The printed text, 4to, 1629,
gives: "With warwolfes and wild cates." Montgomerie's Poems,
ed. D. Cranstoun, S.T.S., 1887, p. 71.

29 "Ane verie excellent and delectabill Treatise intitulit Philotus,"
often ascribed but quite doubtfully to the poet Robert Semple,
who is sometimes sought to be identified with Robert, Lord
Semple. Philotus was printed 4to, 1603, for Robert Charteris,
and again 4to, 1612, for Andrew Hart. Both at Edinburgh. The
plot is from the story Of Phylotus and Emelia, the eighth tale in
Barnaby Rich's Riche his Farewell to Militarie profession, 1581.
I have used the reprint of Philotus for the Bannatyne Club,
ed. J. W. Mackenzie, Edinburgh, 1835. When John Pinkerton
included Philotus in his Scotish Poems, 3 vols, 1792 (vol. iii,
pp. 1–63), he omitted two lines which he considered obscene.
Mackenzie, with some hesitation, printed these, since they were
"overshadowed by the decent veil of Gothic characters."

30 Philotus, E 2, 124.

31 Sibbald, Chronicle of Scottish Poetry, 1802, vol. iv, Glossary, or
An Explanation of Ancient Scottish Words, s.v. Warwolf.

32 Cf. tréow-loga, wed-loga.

33 Folio, Lipsiae, 1737.

34 Operae Horarum subcisivarum, Frankfort, 1615, i, pp. 327 and
328. "Eosque Germani Berwolff, Galli autem Loupe garoux
uocant"; and "lupi noxi . . . Germanis Berwolff".

35 Schambach and Müller, Niederländische Sagen, Göttingen,
1855, p. 182.

36 Op. cit., pp. 1880–1.

37 iii Band 2. Strassburg, 1898, xi, Mythologie, pp. 272–4, sections

31–3. Mogk in a footnote (p. 272, n. 1) has: "Kögel meint dass diese Ableitung falsch sei: ahd. *weriwolf, älter *wariwulf gehöre zu got. wasjan, 'kleiden.'"

38 Halle, 1872–1882, p. 1130.

39 Christiana, 1850, p. 30.

40 verr = a man; úlfr, a wolf.

41 Icelandic-English Dictionary, Gudbrand Vigfusson. Oxford, 1874, p. 680.

42 Ibid., p. 236. Hamr = a shape, and is connected with the phrase skipta hömum "shape-shifting". Ham-klepya is a witch travelling in hamfarir. For a vivid description of this see Yunglinga Saga, lives of the mythical kings of Sweden from Odin to the monarchs of historical days. The work is by Snorri Sturluson (1178–1241), who drew upon the Heimskringla. Úlf-hamr "Wolf's-skin" becomes the name of a legendary prince.

43 E. Littré, Dictionnaire de la Langue Française, tome ii, Première partie, 1869, p. 350.

44 T. iv, 1885, p. 236.

45 A quotation from the Miracles de Notre Dame of Gautier de Coinsi (1177–1236), sometime Prior of Saint-Médard de Soissons. This Abbey, originally founded in 557 by Clotaire I to receive the body of S. Médard, was regarded as the chief Benedictine house in France. In 1131 the church, having been partially pulled down and rebuilt, was reconsecrated by Pope Innocent II, who then granted those visiting this sanctuary indulgences known as "S. Médard's pardons".

46 Godefroy also draws attention to the word varol as used to designate the fish loup (Labrax lupus), the marine bass. Cotgrave (1611) has: "Lubin: A Base, or Sea-Wolfe." For Guernsey, also see Sir Edgar MacCulloch, Guernsey Folk Lore, 1903, p. 230.

47 Vellum; late thirteenth century, small 4to. Twelve lays are attributed to Marie de France (about 1250), and professedly translated from lays of Brittany. The prologue of 56 lines is addressed to a king, probably Henry III of England. The third

lay is Bisclaveret in 318 lines, ff. 131b–133b, col. 2.

48 p. 585. See also Jacques Pelletier, Dialogue de l'Ortografie e Prononciation Françoese, Poitiers, 1550, p. 165, p. 197 and passim.

49 Ed. Lyon, 1593, pp. 222–3.

50 I have used the edition On les Vend a Paris par Philippe le Noir libraire demourant en la rue sainct Jacques a senseigne de la rose blanche couronee (no date, c. 1515, Bodley; Douce, pp. 211). There are extant more than forty MSS. of the Livre de la Chasse, which was printed by Antoine Vérard c. 1507, by Jean Treperel about the same date, and by Philippe le Noir c. 1515.

51 Bodley MS. 546, p. 35, verso (olim Digby MS. 182; vi). The book, written at the beginning of the fifteenth century, is dedicated to Henry, Prince of Wales, son of Henry IV.

52 Aix (no date), s.v. loup-garou.

53 José de Lacerda, Novo Diccionario, Lisboa, 1866.

54 Hertz, Der Werwolf, p. 89, incorrectly says that for "werwolf… im Spanischen ist kein besonderes Wort vorhanden". y Pidal, in answer to my inquiry, writes: "La palabra a que usted se refiere, en español debe ser lobombre. 'Plinio … diz que este que siempre eymos contar en las fabliellas que los omnes se tornan lobos et llaman los lobombres e despues se mudan en omnes, que non lo deuemos creer." General Estoria, pág. 559a. "De si los lobos pueden criar un niño, Kunst da dos obras didácticas y dos leyendas sacadas de manuscritos de la Biblioteca de El Escorial.—Bibliófilos españoles, Madrid, 1878, con bibliografía, pag. 136 n.'"

55 Homer, Odyssey, x, 212–13.

56 Ed. Joh. G. Schneider, 1775, for which see later.

57 iii, 16. "On Lycaon, or Lycanthropia." See The Seven Books of Paulus Ægineta, translated with a Commentary by Francis Adams; the Sydenham Society, 3 vols, 1844, vol. i, pp. 389–90.

58 The physician Haly Abbas (Theor., ix, 7; Pract., v, 24) designates lycanthropia as melancholia canina. Alsaharavius (Pract., i, 2, 28) also seems to allude to the disease as melancholia canina.

The Arabian term is cutubut.

59 Ioannis Tzetzae, Historiarum Variarum Chiliades, ed.
Theophilus Kiesslingius, Lipsiae, 1826, Chil. i, Hist. xix, Περὶ
Βόος τοῦ Μίνωος, Il. 487–9 (p. 21).

ΠασιΟαή. . . .

Μινώταυρον γεγέννηκε βοάνθρωπον θηρίον.

60 λνκανθρωπία appears in a medical writer, Aetius, A.D. 500.
Opera, Venetiis, 1534; 6, 11. Issacius Theophanes, A.D. 817, uses
λυκάνθρωπος as an adjective meaning wolfish, savage, cruel.
Opera, Bonnae, 1839; 745, 13.

61 The Discouerie of Witchcraft, edition 1930, "with an
introduction by the Rev. Montague Summers," p. 52.

62 A Dictionary of the English Language, folio, 1755, vol. ii.

63 J. G. von Hahn, Griechische und albanesische Märchen,
Leipzig, 1864; ii, pp. 189–90.

64 Actually many derivations have been suggested, but we may (I
think) take this as certain. Such a theory as that propounded
by Oeconomos, who suggested that Callicantzaros might have
some connection with the Latin "caligatus" or "calcatura", is
frankly impossible. Nor is Bernard Schmidt's reference (p. 144,
n. 2) to the Turkish karakondjolos, a black scullion slave, a
whit more tenable, although it is true that in J. D. Kieffer and
T. X. Bianchi's Dictionnaire Turc-Français, Paris, 1837, t. ii, p.
469, we have: "qara qondjolos. Loup-garou ou autre monstre
imaginaire, cauchemar." The adjective qara meaning black also
bears the signification "De mauvais augure". See also Hermann
Vámbéry, Etymologisches Wörterbuch der Turko-Tatarischen
Sprachen, Leipzig, 1878; pp. 79, 80 (n. 84). Coräes ("Ατακτα, iv,
p. 211) made the word a compound of καλός and κάνθαρος,
which, however satisfactory in etymological formation, will
not bear anything resembling the sense required. Polites once
wrote (in Πανδώρα, 1866, xvi, p. 453) that as καλλικάντζαρος
is allied to λυκοκάντζαρος, this latter word may contain two
elements, λύκος = "wolf" and κάνθαρος = "beetle". He has,
however, abandoned this view, and later inclined to suggest

that the obscure dialect form καλιτσάγγαρος, found in some villages on the western shores of the Black Sea, is derived from τσαγγάρης "a boot-make", and for the second element either καλίκι "a hoof" or καλός "fine". It is true that the Callicantzaros is in popular tradition often supposed to have hoofs, the feet of an ass or a goat, but the derivation put forward by Polites appears altogether too far-fetched and unreal.

65 Vol. ii, p. 434.

66 Ibid., vol. i, p. 46.

67 Ibid., vol. ii, p. 101.

68 Wien, 1886, p. 380.

69 Ibid., p. 374.

70 Modern Greek Folklore and Ancient Greek Religion, 1910, p. 379.

71 Bernhard Schmidt, Das Volksleben der Neugriechen und das Hellenische Alterhum, Leipzig, 1871, pp. 159–60.

72 Ibid., p. 159, n. 2.

73 Mannhardt's Zeitschrift f. d. Mythol. und Sitternk., iv, 195.

74 Otia Imperialia, ed. Felix Liebrecht, Hanover, 1856, p. 4.

75 Paris, 1844, t. i, p. 69.

76 See Bodin, Démonomanie des Sorciers, ii, 6; ed. Lyon, 1593, pp. 219–20. Also Weyer, vi, 13, De Magorum Infamium Poenis. Opera omnia, Amstedolami, 1660, pp. 494–7.

77 Op. cit., pp. 379–80.

78 Op. cit., Grec. Français, vol. i, 1908, p. 727.

79 "See how he can change his skin when he likes!" 1. 123.

80 Petronius. Tertium edidit Buecheler. Berolini, 1895, 62, p. 41.

81 Metamorphoseon, II, xxii. Recensuit J. van der Vlict. Lipsiae, 1887, pp. 38–9. Plautus in the Persa, ii, 2, 48, uses versipellus of the hair turning grey; "Ne ubi capillus versipellis fiat, foede semper servias," says Sophoclidisca to Paegnium. [Another reading has versicapillus.] In the Bacchides, iv, 4, 11. 658–9, the word is employed with the secondary signification "skilled in dissimulation", "shifty".

vorsipellem frugi convenit esse hominem,

pectus quoi sapit.

"A chap that's worth anything, a fellow who is smart and knowing, has to be able to change his skin," is the maxim of the slave Chrysalus. Cf. modern Italian, versipelle, Prudentius, Cathemeron, ix, 91–2, writes:—

Quid tibi, profane serpens, profiut rebus nouis
Plasma primum perculisse uersipelli astutia?

The same poet, Apotheosis, Praefatio, 26, has the line: "Hae uersipelli astutiæ!"

82 The narrative first occurs in Greek among the works of S. John Damascene. It may be found in the Latin version in the Vitae Patrum, compiled by Héribert Rosweyde, S.J., ed. folio, Lugduni, 1617, pp. 186–259. See also Migne P.G., xcvi, pp. 857–1246.

83 1535–1581. The Latin versions by this great scholar of S. Gregory Nazianzen, S. John Damascene, S. John Chrysostom, and other doctors are famous.

84 Migne P.G., xcvi, pp. 1141–2.

85 Ibid., pp. 1149–1150.

86 Flores Caluinistici, Neapoli, 1585, p. 23.

87 First printed at Lyons, no date, c. 1490.

88 De lamiis, Basil, 1577, c. xiv.

89 Glossarium mediae et infimae Latinitatis, ed. 1885, vol. v, p. 155.

90 Lexicon, ed. De Vit., Prato, 1875. Forcellini defines versipellis as "che muta pelle o faccia". He also draws attention to versipellis = a chameleon.

91 Lexicon (Recueil de Mots de la Basse Latinité), 1866, Migne.

92 Lyons, Sumptibus Claudii Bourgeat.

93 Konrad Maurer, Die Bekehrung des Norwegischen Stammes zum Christenthume, 2 vols, München, 1856, vol. ii, pp. 101–10.

94 G. F. Abbott, Macedonian Folklore, 1903.

95 H. F. Tozer, Researches in the Highlands of Turkey, 2 vols., 1869 (vol. ii, pp. 80 sqq.). Arthur and Albert Schott, Walachische Märchen, Stuttgart and Tübingen, 1845.

96 Ernst Marno, Reisen im Gebeite des blauen und weissen Nil,

Vienna, 1874, pp. 239 sqq. Life and Adventures of Nathaniel Pearce, 1831. Ed. by J. J. Halls, vol. i, p. 288 n. Mansfield Parkyns, Life in Abyssinia, 1868, pp. 300–1, 310–12.

97 P, B. Chaillu, Explorations and Adventures in Equatorial Africa, 1861. D. and C. Livingstone, Narrative of an Expedition to the Zambesi and its Tributaries, 1865, p. 159. Theophilus Waldmeier, Autobiography, 1886. Basset, Les Apocryphes Éthiopiens, iv, 24, 1894. Mary H. Kingsland, Travels in West Africa, 1897, pp. 536–9. T. J. Allridge, The Sherbro and the Hinterland, 1901. H. J. Beatty, Human Leopards, 1915. M. de Lembray, The werewolf of the Africans. Cf. also John Cameron Grant, The Ethiopian, "A Narrative of the Society of Human Leopards," Paris, 1900.

98 G. A. Wilken, De Indische Gids, 1884, pp. 945–50. W. Crooke, The Popular Religion and Folklore of Northern India, 1896, pp. 354–5. W. W. Skeat, Malay Magic, 1900. W. W. Skeat, Fables and Folklore from an Eastern Front, 1901, p. 26. Bezemer, Volksdichtung aus Indonesien, 1904, pp. 363–5, 422–3. Bompas, Folklore of the Santal Parganas, pp. 229, 256.

99 Herbert A. Giles, Strange Stories from a Chinese Studio, 2 vols., 1880; 2nd ed., 1 vol., 1909. The stories are from Liao chai chih i, by P'u Sung-ling. Fox possession in Japan; Captain F. Brinkley, Japan, vol. v (p. 197 sqq.), Oriental Series, 1902, Boston and Tokyo. J. J. M. de Groot, The Religious System of China, Leyden (1907). Dr. M. W. de Visser, "The Fox and the Badger in Japanese Folklore," Transactions of the Asiatic Society in Japan, xxxvi, part 3, 1908. E. T. C. Werner, Myths and Legends of China, 1922. G. Willoughby-Meade, Chinese Ghouls and Goblins, London, 1928, chap. v, pp. 102–138.

100 A. C. Krujt, "De weerwolf bij de Toradja's van Midden-Celebes." Tijdschrift voor Indische Taal- Land- en Volkenkunde, xli (1899), pp. 548–551, 557–560.

101 M. G. Lewis, Journal of a West India Proprietor, 1834, p. 295.

102 Henry R. Schoolcraft, Indian Tribes of the United States, Philadelphia, 1853–6, v, p. 683.

103 Joseph de Acosta, S.J., Historia Natural y Moral de las Indias. Libro septimo, cap. 19. Sevilla, 1590, pp. 499–501. English translation by Edward Grimston, Hakluyt Society reprint, 1880, vol. ii, pp. 497–9. Also Eusèbe Salverte, Des Sciences Occultes, 3rd ed., 1856, c. xiii, pp. 215–17 (English translation, Occult Sciences, 2 vols., 1846).

104 Reise in Brasilien, von Joh. Bapt. von Spix und Carl. Fredr. Phil. von Martius. München, 1823–1831, 3 vols. English translation, Travels in Brazil, 2 vols., 1824, book iv, c. 2, vol. ii, p. 243. Granada, Reseña Histéricodescriptiva de Supersticiones del Rio de la Plata, 1896, pp. 581–627. Ambrosetti, La Leyenda del Yaguareté-Abá, Buenos Aires, 1896; Globus, Illustrierte Zeitschrift für Länder- und Völkerkunde, lxx [1896], pp. 272–3.

105 T. C. Bridges, "Witchcraft To-day," Occult Review, xlv, No. 5, May, 1927, p. 330.

106 Encyclopædia Britannica, ed. 1883, vol. xv, "Lycanthropy," p. 89.

107 Dr. N. Parker, Journal of Mental Science, 1854, p. 52.

108 Dr. Daniel Hach Tuke, Dictionary of Psychological Medicine, 1892, vol. ii, pp. 752–5.

109 "Si ex cholera tunc vocatur proprie mania, et sunt cum saltu et furore et lupinositate, et cum terribili aspectu, et appellatur a quibusdam daemonium lupinum." De Passionibus Capitis, Particula ii, xix. Lilium Medecinae, Lugduni, 1573 (p. 211). Bernard de Gordon, died about 1320.

110 Opera omnia, 2 vols., folio. Lugduni, 1658, vol. i, p. 377.

111 The Nation, New York, 22nd August, 1895.

112 S. Matthew, iv, 24; viii, 16; ix, 32, 33; xii, 22; xv, 22–8; S. Mark, i, 32, 34, 39; iii, 11, 12; ix, 14–28; S. Luke, iv, 41; vi, 18; vii, 21; viii, 27–39; xi, 14; xiii, 32; and elsewhere in the Gospels. See also Montague Summers, The History of Witchcraft, 1926, chapter vi, "Diabolic Possession," pp. 198–275.

113 Practica Medicina, Lib. i, pars ii, cap. xvi. Opera omnia, Parisiis, 1641, t. i, p. 158.

114 S. John, ix, 3.

115 Guazzo, Compendium Maleficarum, 1608, i, 6. English translation by E. A. Ashwin, edited by Montague Summers, 1929 (p. 17).

116 Daemonolatreia, folio, 1595, iii, 6. English translation by E. A. Ashwin, edited by Montague Summers, 1930 (pp. 161–3). See also Guazzo, op. cit., II, xiii.

117 Opera omnia, Parisiis, 1641, folio, t. iii, pp. 1126–1157.

118 For the life of Sennert (and other physicians of whom mention is made in this chapter) see N. F. J. Eloy, Dictionnaire Historique de la Médicine, 4 vols., Mons, 1778, under the several names.

119 L'Incredulité Sçavante et la Credulité Ignorante au suiet des Magiciens et des Sorciers, Lyon, 1678. Seconde Partie; discours vii, pp. 474–5.

120 Apud Migne, Patres Graeci, vol. x, p. 1338, B.

121 Dæmonologie, 1597, ii, 5 (Bodley; Douce, i, 230). Reprint ed. G. B. Harrison, 1924.

122 Ecclesiasticus, xxxix, 33.

123 See Pliny, Historia Naturalis, vii, 2: "In eadem Africa familias quasdam effascinantium, Isigonus et Nymphodorus tradunt, quarum Iaudatione intereant probata, arescant arbores, emoriantur infantes." Also Aulus Gellius, ix, 4. Cf. R. C. Maclagan, Evil Eye in the Western Highlands, 1902, pp. 7–9, 116–18. The danger of over-praising and excessive admiration is common knowledge.

124 These methods are fully discussed by all the great authorities, and there is a universal consensus of opinion that witches can and do cast spells in these ways, practices which still endure. Boguet, Discours des Sorciers, English translation An Examen of Witches, by E. A. Ashwin, edited by Montague Summers, 1929, has five chapters: xxv, "Whether Witches kill by their Blowings and their Breath"; xxvi, "Whether Witches afflict with Words"; xxvii, "Whether Witches afflict with Looking"; xxviii, "How Witches afflict with the Hand"; and xxix, "How Witches afflict with a Wand" (pp. 75–86). Paul Grilland, also, in his De

sortilegiis, has an important chapter, viii, "Maleficium potest solis verbis perfici," apud Malleus Maleficarum, Lyon, 1669, tom. ii, pars. ii, pp. 282–3. Leonard Vair's work, De Fascino, Parisiis, 1583, should be consulted, especially c. iii, "De visu qui Fascini diffinitionem impeditur" (pp. 11–16); iv, "De tactu Fascinum efficiente" (pp. 17–21), and v, "De vocis natura quae Fascini causa exstitit" (pp. 21–6). The whole subject of fascinatio, which he happily defines as contagio seu infectis (p. 29), is discussed at length by Delrio, Disquisitionum Magicarum, Liber iii, pars. 1, quaestio 3, ed. 1603, t. ii, pp. 26–83, De Maleficio hostili.

125 Op. cit., iii, discours xvi (p. 801).

126 S. Matthew, iv, 8, 9.

127 For this phrase see Reginald Scott, The discouerie of witchcraft, 1584, iii, 15; reprinted with Introduction by Montague Summers, 1930, pp. 36–7. T. Higgins, Junius' Nomenclator (1585), has "Fascinus, a bewitching or eyebiting", and Phillips (1658) notes: "eyebite to fascinate or bewitch from a certain evil influence from the eye." T. Ady, A Candle in the Dark (1656), ii, 104, derives from Scott. See also Rev. St. John D. Seymour, Irish Witchcraft and Demonology, 1913, p. 68.

128 S. Thomas, Contra Gentiles, iii, 103, and Summa, i, 117, 3; Malleus; Bl. Angelo, Summa angelica, Superstitio, 5; "multiplex experientia docet" (ed. folio, 1515, Strassburg, fo. ccxxxiii).

129 The terrible power of the Evil Eye is so general and so potent, that I have thought it well to give ample annotations on this passage so that those who wish to pursue the subject further may be helped in their investigations. For general works see: Leonard Vair, De Fascino, Libri Tres, Parisiis, 1583, i, e. 3, pp. 11–16; Fromann, Tractatus de fascinatione novus et singularis, Norimbergae, 1675; Elworthy, The Evil Eye, London, 1895 (to be used with caution as to the author's conclusions); R. C. Maclagan, Evil Eye in the Western Highlands, 1902; Seligmann, Der böse Blick, Berlin, 1910; Westermarck, Ritual and Belief in Morocco, 1926, vol. i, pp. 414–478.

130 Oldenberg, Die Religion des Vedas, Berlin, 1894, pp.
    482, 502 sqq.
131 Vendîdâd, Oxford, 1895, xix, 6, 45 (141); xx, 3 (12).
132 Arist., Probl., xx, 34. The charm was broken by spitting thrice.
    Theocritus, vi, 39, a passage quoted by Diogenianus, Prov., iv,
    82. Cf. also Theocritus, xx, 12, and Tibullus, I, ii, 100. There is
    a famous reference in Vergil, Eclogues, iii, 103. Aulus Gellius,
    xvi, 12, 3, has: "Item fascinum appellat [Cloatius Verus], quasi
    bascanum, et fascinare esse quasi bascinare." Curtius rejects
    this connection of fascinare with βασκαίνειν, but it is accepted
    by Corssen, ii, p. 257. Professor Robinson Ellis, Commentary
    on Catullus, 1889, vii, 12 (p. 25), suggests that the notion of
    witchcraft was originally that of the evil tongue rather than
    the evil eye. Cf. βάζευν, Οάσκειν. Compare The Witch of
    Edmonton by Ford, Dekker, and Rowley, 4to, 1658 (acted 1623),
    ii, when Mother Sawyer says:—
Some call me witch . . .
Urging that my bad tongue—by their bad usage made so—
Forspeaks their cattle . . .
Cf. Pliny, Historia Naturalis, vii, 2, and (of the catoblepas and
    basilisk) viii, 21. See also Jahn, "Über den Aberglauben
    des bösen Blicks bei den Alten," in Berichte über die
    Verhandlungen der Königlich-Sächsisten Gesellschaft der
    Wissenschaften zu Leipzig, Philologisch-historische Classe,
    xvii. Leipzig, 1855, p. 63 sqq.
133 Andree, Ethnographische Parallelen und Vergleiche, Stuttgart,
    1878, pp. 41 sqq.
134 Feilberg, "Der böse Blick in Nordischen Uberlieferung,"
    in Zeitschrift des Vereins für Volksunde, xi (Berlin,
    1901), p. 305 sqq.
135 E. W. Lane, Manners and Customs of the Modern Egyptians, 2
    vols., 1838, c. xi. Gardiner, "The Evil Eye in Egypt," Proceedings
    of the Society of Biblical Archœology, xxxviii, London,
    1916, p. 129 sqq.
136 Campbell Thompson, Semitic Magic (London, 1908), p. 88.

137 Ludgwig Blau, Das jüdische Zauberwesen, Strassburg,
   1898, p. 153 sqq.
138 C. R. Conder, Heth and Moab, 1883, p. 295.
139 Koran, cxiii, 1, 2, 5; et alibi. Mishkāt, xxi, 1, 2. English
   translation by Matthews, Calcutta, 1810, vol. ii, p. 377.
140 J. Mactaggart, Gallovidian Encyclopœdia, 1824, 2nd ed.,
   London, 1876, persons suspected of having "an ill ee". James
   Kelly, Scottish Proverbs, London, 1721 (and 1818), cites, "God
   saine your eye, man." R. C. Maclagan, Evil Eye in the Western
   Highlands, 1902.
141 J. C. Lawson, Modern Greek Folklore, 1910, pp. 8–15. Special
   forms of prayer, commonly known as βασκανισμοὶ, are
   provided for those who have been blinked by the evil eye.
   Margaret Hardie, "The Evil Eye in some Greek Villages of the
   Upper Haliakmon Valley in West Macedonia," in Journal of the
   Royal Anthropological Institute, London, 1923, liii, p. 160 sqq.
   For Albania see George Borrow, Zincali, 2 vols., London, 1841,
   part i, c. 8.
142 "I do not exaggerate when I affirm, at all events, my own
   persuasion that two-thirds of the total inhabitants of the
   Tamar side implicitly believe in the power of the mal' occhio,
   as the Italians name it, or the evil eye." Rev. Robert Hawker,
   of Morwenstow, Cornwall, in Mrs. Whitcombe's Bygone
   Days in Devon and Cornwall, 1873, p. 139. See Blakeborough,
   Wit, Character, Folk-lore and Customs of the North Riding
   of Yorkshire, London, 1898, for northerly beliefs as regards
   the evil eye. Word-Lore, vol. i, 1926, pp. 125–6, has a modern
   example of overlooking in an English village. Cf. letters in The
   Times from Mr. Andrew Innes of Kendal and Mr. R. Tristram
   of Witney, 20th and 22nd September, 1930. Also "Spells of the
   Evil Eye" in Cornwall, Mr. W. H. Paynter, Daily Express, 26th
   September, 1930. In the West Country it is believed that to kiss
   a corpse renders one immune from being blinked, see Sunday
   Dispatch, 24th April, 1932.
143 Westermarck, Ritual and Belief in Morocco, 1926, vol. i, pp.

414–478. This great authority quotes the current saying: "One half of mankind dies from the evil eye."

144 Oric Bates, The Eastern Libyans, 1914, p. 180 sqq.

145 R. W. Felkin, "Notes on the Waganda Tribe of Central Africa," in Proceedings of the Royal Society of Edinburgh, 1884–6, xiii, p. 760.

146 Mitford, Through the Zulu Country, London, 1883, p. 317.

147 W. H. I. Bleek, Brief Account of Bushmen Folklore, 1875, pp. 10, 14.

148 Seligmann, op. cit., i, p. 42 sqq. Andree, op. cit., p. 39 sqq.

149 Seligmann, op. cit., i, p. 43 sqq.

150 Bullen, Forty Years in New Zealand, London, 1876. George Turner, Samoa, a Hundred Years ago and long before, London, 1884, p. 23.

151 Seligmann, op. cit., i, 44 sqq. Andree, op. cit., p. 35.

152 To deal with Italy and Spain at all adequately would require a veritable chapter of notes alone. The counter-charms against the evil eye and similar fascinations must be familiar to any traveller who has visited these two countries, and indeed to most others beside. The subject in all its bearings is of enormous interest, but demands ample treatment or a mere mention.

153 The Essayes . . . Newly enlarged, 1625. Of Enuy, ix, p. 40. "The Act of Enuy," p. 47. Bodley: Arch. Bodi. D. 104 [Glass case, 21].

154 Sennert derives this from the Commentary on Apuleius of Filippo Beroaldo of Bologna, 1453–1505. The Commentary is printed in the works of Apuleius, Basileae, 3 vols., 8vo, 1620. The phrase in question occurs in book iv, 26, of the Metamorphoseon: "sic ad instar Athracidis vel Protesilai dispestae disturbataeque sunt nuptiae," says the captured maiden. [Van der Vlict following the codex Florentinus reads "Attidis", Metamorphoseon, Lipsiae (Teubner), 1887, i, p. 88 with note.] Atracis is Hippodamia, the Thessalian woman, Ovid, Amores, I, iv, 8; Heroides, xvii, 248. She is called "Atracia virgo" by Valerius Flaccus, i, 141. Atracia ars is the Thessalian

art, that is magic, from Atrax (now Sidhiro-peliko), a town in
Thessaly on the Peneus. Cf. Statius, Thebais, i, 105–6:
Phoebes
Atracia rubet arte labor.
"Athracie est magica scientia." See Lactantius (who must not be
confused with the Christian writer), Bernatius, and others who
gloss this passage. Cf. Valerius Flaccus, vi, 447.

155 Lamb's splendid phrase on The Witch of Middleton will
be readily remembered: "The witches of Middleton are fine
creations. Their power too is in some measure over the mind.
They raise jars, jealousies, strifes, like a thick scurf o'er life."

156 Westermarck, op. cit., i, pp. 571–3, speaks of the witchcraft
affecting men with sexual impotence, called in Morocco
"tsqāf", and much dreaded.

157 See Montague Summers, The Geography of Witchcraft, 1927,
ch. vii, pp. 531–7.

158 Malleus, part ii, question i, c. vii: "How [Witches], as it were, .
. . Deprive Man of his Virile Member." English tr. by Montague
Summers, 1928, pp. 118–122.

159 George Giffard, A Dialogue concerning Witches and
Witchcraftes, 1593, records the popular belief in England:
"the witches haue their spirits, . . . some in one likenesse, and
some in another, as like cattes, weasils, toads, or mise," B.
4 verso. There are several references to mice as familiars in
the statements of Hopkins' assistant, John Sterne, but these
examinations are very suspect. E.g. "The impe which the said
Joyce Boanes sent was a dund one like a mouse." Howell, State
Trials, v, 834.

160 "This example of Job is not fit to prove that a godly man may
be bewitched, seeing the deuill is not sayde to deale by witches
against him, but it doeth prooue, that not only the godlie,
but euen the most godly (as holy Job, who had none like him
upon earth) may for their triall be giuen into the handes of
Satan to be afflicted and tempted." Giffard, op. cit., D. 4 recto.
There is something of a quibble here, for all must agree that

79

Deo permittente the Devil is the agent, whether directly or mediately by a witch.

161 Op. cit., partie iii, discours 2, p. 691.

162 See for a more extended treatment of these details Pietro Piperno, De Magicis Affectibus, Benevento, 1634, lib. iii and iv, pp. 79–136.

163 "Haec difficultas non est parir momenti." José Angles, Flores Theologicarum Quaestionum in II Sent., Madriti, 1586, p. 377.

164 Ven. Duns Scotus, Opus Oxoniense, In 4 Sent., d. 34. Blessed Henry of Segusio (Summa aurea), Godfrey of Fontaines (XIV Quodlibeta), Ubertino, are quoted in the Malleus, Eng. trans., p. 157. For Guazzo see the Compendium, iii, 1, Eng. trans., 1929, pp. 163–4.

165 S. Thomas (Summa, ii, 2, q. 78), S. Bonaventura, Peter a Palude, S. Albertus Magnus, are quoted in the Malleus, loc. cit., p. 158. For Boguet see Examen, ch. xxxvi, Eng. tr., 1929, pp. 111–14.

166 Comprising pp. 336–379.

167 Ibid., p. 377.

168 Ibid., pp. 378–9. De Arte magica. Artie. vi. Tertia diffic. "Licelitne bona fide magicis incantationibus, & adjurationibus uti?" Conclusio. "Haud licet."

169 Father Stephen Donovan, O.F.M., writes in the Catholic Encyclopœdia, vol. i, s.n. Angelo Carletti di Chivasso, that in the Summa "one is impressed with the gravity and fairness that characterized [Blessed Angelo's] opinions throughout". The Summa was written, to use the author's own words, "pro utilitate . . . eorum qui cupiunt laudabiliter vivere," and even to-day acclaimed as "a most valuable guide in matters of conscience".

170 1280–1322. (The date of death is also given as 1330, and also 1345.) There is a good edition of the Commentarium, Rome, 1596–1605.

171 S. Augustine's exact words are: "Qui utitur fide illius quem constat jurasse per deos falsos, et utitur non ad malum, sed ad licitum et bonum, non peccato ejus se sociat quo per daemonia

juravit, sed bono pacto ejus quo fidem servavit." Epistola xlvii
(a) ad Publicolam. Migne, P.L., t. xxxiii, S. Augustini Opera,
vol. ii, p. 185 (2).

172 Summa Angelica de Casibus conscientie, folio, 1515. Impensis
Joannis Knoblouch. Superstitio, fo. ccxxxiii, 13.

173 pp. 138–150.

174 Ibid., pp. 144–5.

175 Eng. tr. (1928), pp. 155–164.

176 Malleus, ed. 1669, t. ii, pars. ii, pp. 185–6.

177 Op. cit., p. 1151.

178 Ed. Moguntiae, 1603, t. iii, pp. 157–172.

179 In IV Sent. libros comment. (Salamanca, 1555–6), d.
34, q. 1, a. 3.

180 Fustis Daemonum, c. v, ad finem, ed. 1604 (Lugduni), p. 11.

181 De Magicis Affectibus, 1634, p. 77.

182 "Unlucky Possessions," by T. C. Bridges. Occult Review,
March, 1927, vol. xlv, No. 3, pp. 159–60.

183 Remy agrees with this, Daemonolatreia, iii, 3. "That there is
nothing which can so quickly and effectively induce Witches
to remove an Evil Spell as Threats and Blows and Violence . . ."
Eng. tr., 1930, pp. 148–154.

184 Casus Conscientiae Benedicti XIV, Dec., 1743, Cas. 111,
Ferrariae, 1764, p. 155.

185 Daily News, 20th January, 1928; Daily Express, 26th August,
1930; Sunday Times, 31st August, 1930.

186 "Magic—Black and White," by William Hichens.
Contemporary Review, August, 1931 (No. 788), p. 248.

187 See The History of Witchcraft, Montague Summers, 1926, c. vi,
pp. 202–224.

188 Piperno, op. cit., p. 53.

189 Suidas, s.v. Μάρκελλος.

190 οὗ βίβλους ἀνέθηκεν ἐϋκτιμένη ἐνὶ Ῥώμη
Ἀδριανὸς προτέρων προθερέστερος ἡγεμονήων
καὶ πας Ἀδριανο ὁ μέγ᾽ ἔξοχος "Αντων νος, ...
Anthologia Palatina, caput vii: Epigrammata Sepulcralia, 158,

ed. Parisiis, 1864, vol. i, p. 302.

191 Marcelli Sidetae Fragmenta, recognovit Maximilianus Schneider, p. 118. Apud "Commentationes Philologiae quibus Ottoni Ribbeckio . . . congratulantur Discipuli". Lipsiae, Teubner, 1888.

192 Πλουτάρχου περὶ τῆς τῶν ἐλευθέρων παιδῶν ἀγωγῆ ς. Accedunt bina ejusdem Plutarchi et Marcelli Sidetae medici fragmenta Graece recensuit Joh. G. Schneider. Argentorati, [Strassburg], 1775, p. 109.

193 Pauli Æginetae Medici Optimi Libreri Septem. Basileae, 1538, per Hieronymum Gemusaeum. [Bodley, D. 1, 6, Med.]

194 Physician and classical scholar, 1796–1861, of whom an account may be found in the D.N.B., vol. i, 1885, pp. 95–6.

195 Op. cit., vol. i, pp. 389–90.

196 The various Greek authors have been collected in Physici et Medici Graeci Minores, ed. Julius Ludovicus Ideler. Berolini, 1841, 2 vols. Nicander's Theriacs, Θηριακά, were edited with a useful commentary by J. G. Schneider, Lipsiae, 1816.

197 See also for the various biographies N. F. J. Eloy, Dictionnaire Historique de la Medicine, 4 vols., Mons, 1778, under the several names.

198 p. 282.

199 Vol. i, pp. 203–243.

200 p. 227.

201 Two vols., Paris, 1876. Avicenna, vol. i, pp. 466–477; Haly Abbas, i, pp. 381–8; Alsaharavius, i, pp. 437–457; and Razis, i, pp. 337–354.

202 Venice, 1588, pp. 291–7.

203 Bononiae, 1583, pp. 339–377.

204 Anatomy of Melancholy, part i, sec. 1, mem. 1, subs. 4.

205 Opera omnia, Amstelodami, 1660, pp. 335–7.

206 pp. 28–33.

207 p. 32.

208 Lilium Medicinae, Lugduni, 1573, p. 213.

209 Basilææ, 1568, pp. 142–3.

210 Francofurti et Lipsiae, folio, 1666, p. 1500.
211 Opera omnia, 4 vols., 1602–6, folio. I have used the ed. Francofurti, 1634, folio.
212 Ibid., p. 348.
213 Omnia opera, Venetiis, folio, 1574, p. 79, verso; caput ix, De lycanthropia.
214 Naples, MDcclxi, tom. ii, pp. 112–13. The Lexicon Medicum Graeco-Latinum was first published at Venice, 8vo, 1607. The edition 8vo, Bale, 1628, is esteemed. The work ran into more than fifteen editions when it was edited by Jacques-Pancrace Brum as Castellus renouatus, Nuremberg, 4to, 1682, after which date it was again very frequently reprinted in its revised form.
215 Op. cit., p. 344.
216 S. Luke, ix, 39.
217 In the collection, Malleus Maleficarum, etc., 4 vols., 1669, vol. iv, p. 13.
218 For Holy Baptism see the Bull of Eugenius IV, Exultate Deo, often referred to as a decree of the Council of Florence; and also the Catechism of the Council of Trent, Session vii, "De Baptismo."
219 Mr. G. L. Kittredge in his Witchcraft in Old and New England, 1928 (p. 237), refers to the Laws of Hammurabi, but is not clear (p. 543) as to the purport of the Babylonian statute. For an account of the ordeal of swimming see The Discovery of Witches, by Montague Summers, Cayme Press, 1928, pp. 35–40.
220 Aethelstan, 11, 23, Liebermann, Die Gesetze des Angelsachsen, i, 162; i, 23; Thorpe, Ancient Laws, folio, 1840, p. 90; cf. also Fuller, Church History, 1656, book ii, century x, ch. 9, p. 127.
221 Daemonologie, 1597, third booke, ch. vi (ad finem). But see Johann Georg Godelmann, De Magis, Veneficis et Lamiis, Francoforti, 1591, lib. iii, v, "De Exploratione per Aquam Frigidam" (iii, pp. 30–45).
222 Chapter vii, sec. 2, p. 208.

223 The Discovery of Witches, by Matthew Hopkins, 1647, Querie 10 (4).

224 See Montague Summers, The Geography of Witchcraft, 1927, c. 11, pp. 178–9.

225 This case is also noticed in Folk-Lore Record, III, ii, 1881, p. 292 (from the Telegraph), and in the Essex Review, v, 1896, p. 159.

226 Op. cit., De Morbis Ventriculi Liber, pp. 439–443, Responsum.

227 De Synodo Diocesana, xiii, c. xvii, 6. Opera omnia, folio, 1767. In Typographia Bassanensi, tom. xii, p. 162.

228 Op. cit., III, vi (ad finem).

229 Part iii, question xv, Eng. tr., p. 227.

230 Tractatus de Sortilegiis, II, vii. Malleus, Lugduni, 1669, ii, pp. 284–5.

231 Demonomanie, iv, 4, ed Lyon, 1593, p. 417.

232 Commentarius in Tit. Codicis, lib. ix, de Maleficis, ed. Treves (H. Bock), 1605, pp. 720–1.

233 Godelmann, op. cit., iii, 3 (p. 18): "Paulus Grillandus, Bodinus & inquisitores, validissimum signum cognoscendi veneficas, & hoc dicunt, quod lachrymas emittere non possunt." Godelmann comments on this and other signs at some length.

234 Delrio, op. cit., v, iv, 25. Ed. Moguntiae, 1603, t. iii, p. 34.

235 Practica, Venice, Giunta, 1557, folio. In Nonum Librum Almansoris Expositio, c. xvi, De melancholia, "oculi ejus sunt sicci . . . non lachrymantes," ut cit. supra.

236 Opera omnia, Parisiis, 1641, t. ii, p. 150.

237 Opera omnia, t. I, II, XV, p. 152, where rabidarum is misprinted rapidarum.

238 De la Folie, 2 ts., Paris, 1845. Tom. i, pp. 87–8. There are other references to lycanthropy in the same volume at pp. 202, 232, 279, 310, 336, and in t. ii at p. 416; pp. 310–344, Dr. Calmiel studies the cases of lycanthropy in the Jura and at Angers. He draws his material from Boguet and De Lanere. The case of Gilles Gamier is noted, pp. 279–283. See also for lycanthropy, Böttiger, Beitr. zur Sprengel's Geschichte der Medezin, bd.

ii, pp. 3–45.

239 1892, vol. ii, pp. 752–5. Dr. Tuke notes that lycanthropy is "somewhat obscure and but little discussed in treatises on mental disorders".

240 ii, p. 58.

241 De Serv. Dei Beatif. et Beat. Canonizatione, lib. iv, Pars. 1, c. xxix. Opera omnia, folio, 1767, pp. 148–152.

www.ingramcontent.com/pod-product-compliance
Lightning Source LLC
Chambersburg PA
CBHW020239030726
47497CB00009B/3163

* 9 7 8 1 4 4 7 4 0 6 3 4 1 *